REKINDLED MAGIC

THE THORNE WITCHES BOOK 5

T.M. CROMER

COPYRIGHT

To all the laid-back and loving men out there:
Thank you for always understanding what your significant
other needs, even when they may not.
You are who I like to call my Quentin Collective;
funny, warm, loving, and steadfast.

ALSO BY T.M. CROMER

Books in The Thorne Witches Series:

SUMMER MAGIC

AUTUMN MAGIC

WINTER MAGIC

SPRING MAGIC

REKINDLED MAGIC

LONG LOST MAGIC

FOREVER MAGIC

ESSENTIAL MAGIC

Books in The Stonebrooke Series:

BURNING RESOLUTION

THE TROUBLE WITH LUST

A LOVE TO CALL MINE (coming soon)

THE BAKERY

EASTER DELIGHTS

HOLIDAY HEART

Books in The Fiore Vineyard Series:

PICTURE THIS

RETURN HOME

ONE WISH

Look for The Holt Family Series starting 2020!

FINDING YOU

THIS TIME YOU

INCLUDING YOU

AFTER YOU

THE GHOST OF YOU

CHAPTER 1

THEN

"*H*ave her home by eleven."

Quentin Buchanan met the frosty gaze of Holly's father, Alastair Thorne, and tried not to gulp. His motto was to never show fear.

"Yes, sir." Quentin wasn't insane enough to think he could challenge a powerful and dangerous warlock of Alastair's caliber. At eighteen, Quentin was still a relative newbie compared to the older man. If Alastair wanted his daughter home by eleven, Quentin figured he'd have her home by ten-forty-five as a precaution.

Holly laughed off Alastair's decree and intertwined her fingers with Quentin's. She tugged him off the porch and toward his black Harley Sportster 1200.

"Oh, you changed the design!" she exclaimed when they were close.

He eyed the twisting turquoise flames and smiled with pride. It had taken him three tries, but he finally managed to conjure paint the exact shade of her gorgeous irises. "Yeah."

Quentin swung one leg over and waited for her to tie up her long chestnut hair. When she was finished, he held out a hand to help her mount behind him. If he took a little extra time to start the bike and rev the engine, only he was to know the stall tactic allowed him to revel in the feel of her full breasts pressed against his back.

His skin prickled, and he sensed he was being watched. Quentin looked toward the porch.

Alastair still stood watching them with his arms crossed over his massive chest.

He knew Quentin's ulterior motive.

Quentin grinned, gunned the engine one more time, and roared away with Holly's arms and legs wrapped tightly around him.

"Where are you taking me?" she shouted.

"You'll see," he hollered in return.

She leaned forward and tucked her chin against his shoulder.

He imagined he could hear her sigh of happiness.

They followed the curve of the two-lane highway for another twenty minutes until they reached the bottom of Yellow Creek Mountain. The only sound was the guttural throbbing of the engine echoing across the night.

Something close to contentment settled in Quentin's chest. He could make a forever-hobby of driving across the country if only Holly was clinging to him. His left palm covered the delicate hands locked across his abdomen. When she laced her fingers with his, his heart stuttered.

She was so trusting and affectionate. The need to protect her, to nourish the love she freely offered, had become ingrained in him.

Instead of heading toward town, Quentin changed direction and drove toward the airport. He circled around the hub and found a dirt road to the left of the smallest terminal.

The road, with its gate clearly marked as "no trespassing," was meant for airport maintenance personnel only. He didn't care and knew Holly wouldn't either. The wild child residing in her five-foot-four frame would thrill to the fact they were breaking the rules.

She didn't speak as he slowed. Anticipating the need, she waved her hand. The lock fell from the chain, and the large metal gate swung wide to allow their entrance. He felt more than heard her laughter. The carefree sound was robust and possessed the ability to curl around his dick and squeeze. It was an intoxicating combination of naughty and happy. Her laugh spoke to his soul.

He parked by the fence line, removed the bungee securing the blanket on the back fender, and led her to the end of the runway. When he'd found the perfect spot, he unfurled the blanket and laid it on the grass.

With an unhurried motion, he relaxed back on his arms and crossed his booted feet at the ankles. He gazed up at her and smiled his invitation.

Holly was beside him in an instant, burrowing between him and his leather jacket.

"Cold?"

"A little," she admitted.

"I'm an idiot. I should've made sure you had a warmer jacket."

"Alastair taught me how to warm my body by manipulating my cells." She glanced up into his face and shrugged. "The chill is a result of the night air. I don't mind it."

"I have the perfect way to warm you," he said suggestively.

"Well, get to warming."

Holly didn't have to ask twice. Quentin had their positions reversed before she could blink. She released a happy giggle, and he chuckled in return.

The V at the top of her thighs cradled his jean-clad hips perfectly. He couldn't prevent the instinctive rub of his pelvis against hers. Somehow, even as tall as he was, they fit as if they'd been made only for each other. From the moment they'd met, he'd known she was the one for him. No other would do.

"We have about ten minutes of make-out time before the next plane takes off," he said.

Wordlessly, she reached her slender arms up and dragged his head down to hers. Their lips met in an explosion of youthful passion. Tongues tangled and teased. Hands explored. Bodies practically fused together in their need. They made out for the entire time.

He could never get enough of touching her. The feel of her silky hair wrapped around his hand. The satiny smoothness of the bare skin of her back and belly. The intoxicating smell of the little spot below her ear where his lips unerringly zeroed in every time they came together.

His watch beeped, and he reluctantly drew away.

Her pout was adorable.

Quentin laughed and tugged her up into a seated position between his legs, the ideal position to wrap his arms around her and cradle her back against his chest. "Watch."

The small passenger plane taxied down the runway and headed directly for their love nest. Holly screamed her delight when it lifted off above their heads. The whining sound of the engines was deafening, but the vibration could be felt on the ground and through his chest.

After the plane was out of sight, she twisted to look up into his grinning face. "That was amazing!"

He agreed. It was almost as exhilarating as having her in his arms.

A swirl of blue lights caught his attention.

Shit! They were busted.

If they got hauled to jail for trespassing, her dad was going to kill him.

"Oh, shit!" she yelled. She followed it up with a sneeze. Within a minute, a small flock of crows settled on the ground around them.

He couldn't see her blush, but he knew it was there. Her reaction was always the same when she forgot and swore. Quentin grinned and gave her a quick squeeze before he waved the birds off with a flick of his wrist.

With a war cry, she scrambled to her feet. "Let's make a run for it!"

Quentin jumped up beside her.

"You're crazy," he laughed. He could've reminded her teleportation was a safer bet, but he didn't care to spoil her fun. "We'll never make it."

"We'll go out like Bonnie and Clyde. They'll never take us

alive!" she shouted with a fist in the air. "We'll go down in the history books."

"You have the soul of a rebel, love." He dropped a soft, lingering kiss on her puffy, ruby lips. "But Alastair would revive me to kill me again if anything happened to you. As it is, I doubt I'll see the sun come up tomorrow."

Two cop cars pulled up about ten yards away. The officers went on, ad nauseam, about punk kids breaking the law. Quentin tuned them out to watch Holly attempt to charm her way out of being hand-cuffed. From his position against the cruiser, he focused on her beau-tiful, animated face.

The grin on his own face had to look as dopey as it felt, but he couldn't contain it. He loved her spirit. He also loved that her hand-cuffs mysteriously dropped to the ground within seconds after they were clicked into place—much to the frustration of the officer who attempted to arrest her.

In a show of unity, he used a surge of magic to unlock and drop his own. They tried to smother their grins against the cool metal of the car when the officers started to malign the handcuff manufacturer after a third attempt to restrain them.

Holly and Quentin were shoved into the back of the squad car, but before Officer Not-So-Friendly could close the door, she propped it open with her booted foot. "Can I bum a cigarette?" She nodded toward the pack on the dashboard. "Getting arrested stresses me out. I need a light."

The older officer released an irritated growl as he slammed the door. Their laughter echoed around the interior of the squad car. Their eyes met, and even though they were in a whole heap of trou-ble, Quentin wouldn't have changed a second of tonight. He suspected she felt the same way when she rested her head on his shoulder and sighed.

"I don't want to be on the other end of the call to your dad when we have to request bail."

"Yeah, he already thinks you're trouble."

"He's going to have to get used to having me around. I intend to marry you, Holly Anne Thorne," he declared huskily.

She snuggled closer.

He rested his cheek on the crown of her head. "I love you," he whispered.

"I love you, too."

A sharp rap on the window brought their heads up. An angry Alastair stood on the other side of the door.

"Oh, shit," she muttered.

Holly sneezed, and Quentin quickly balled his hand to stop the influx of birds.

"It's official. He's going to kill me," he said in a low voice. "How do you suppose he got here so quickly?"

"The sheriff is a Thorne."

"Great. I'm going to rot in jail."

She laughed and bumped his shoulder with hers. "I'll spring you from the joint."

"I think you're an outlaw at heart, love."

She giggled, and his suspicions were confirmed.

CHAPTER 2

NOW

"What are you doing here?"

Holly's surly tone set Quentin's teeth on edge, but he hid his irritation—as he had for nine years. "Hello, my love."

She rolled her eyes as she always did when he used that particular endearment. Quentin stifled a laugh. An irate Holly amused him. Her turquoise-blue eyes would deepen exactly three shades darker, and her full mouth would compress in a tight, white line. When that happened, a dimple would appear on her left cheek. The dimple never failed to fascinate him.

"Don't you have a job or hobby?" she asked as she returned to the task on her computer.

"My job is you," he replied as he leaned his elbows on the counter.

"The stalking is getting old, Quentin."

"Who's stalking? I'm guarding you."

"Pfft. Well, if you're going to linger, there is a pallet of pet food that needs to be stocked on those shelves." She used her chin to indicate the shelving unit to her left without removing her eyes from the screen.

"Your wish is my command, my prickly pear."

For the second time in as many minutes, she graced him with an eye roll. He grinned and whistled a jaunty tune on his way to the stockroom. He passed Holly's twin sister, Summer, who also happened to be the doctor of record here at the clinic. "Hello, gorgeous."

"Hello, tease."

Quentin laughed because Summer and her other three sisters already knew what Holly failed to realize. He may *seem* like a player, but he was, in truth, a one-woman man. He'd never stopped loving Holly, and as far as he was concerned, no one else would ever hold his heart.

The hand truck was easy to locate. After a quick check to make sure he was alone, he waved a hand to lighten the weight of the larger bags. No sense breaking his back if he didn't have to.

Quentin stacked the feed to the top of the hand truck and returned to the waiting area of the Thorne Veterinary Clinic to stock shelves. As he bent for the fifth time to retrieve a bag, he felt the eyes of the multiple female employees upon him. From his peripheral vision, he noted Holly was one of the gawkers, and he bit the inside of his cheek to suppress his self-satisfied smile.

"Pace yourselves, ladies. I have another pallet to stock," he teased.

Their amused titters met with a low grumble.

Quentin lost his playful air and met Holly's livid stare. A large part of him was pleased she'd become territorial. However, an even larger part knew she'd never act on her feelings for him.

A long time ago, their relationship had been damaged by lies. Lies crafted by Holly's best friend, Michelle Wright, to make it appear he'd cheated on Holly. He never did. But Michelle had been a consummate actress and played on Holly's insecurities.

Sadness consumed him from out of the blue. They'd lost nearly ten years to Michelle's games, and the way things currently stood between him and Holly, they were likely to lose another ten or more.

Quentin presented his back and continued to stock the retail shelves, not trusting his ability to maintain the faux carefree air when he was feeling anything but today. He'd come to a decision about his future.

When they found the last of the artifacts for Alastair to resurrect Holly's mother, Quentin would hit the road. Holly's family unit would be restored, and his protection would be unnecessary. It was long past time for him to move on.

A small hand on his forearm made him jump. "Mister?"

A tiny, black-haired sprite of about six or seven stood beside him. She gazed up at him with large liquid pools of anguish. Quentin's heart contracted. The angst in the child's expression reminded him of Holly when she was in pain.

He squatted in front of the girl and smiled gently. "What can I do for you, little lady?"

"My dog... Mama needs help," she cried tearfully.

A glance at the window showed a woman struggling to pick up an overweight Rottweiler from the back seat of her car. He pointed to Holly. "See that woman over there?" When the girl nodded, he said, "You go tell her to prepare a room. I'll help your mom."

She nodded again and ran across the reception area toward Holly.

Quentin didn't wait but charged outside to relieve the child's mother of her burden. "I've got him."

"Thank you! Bear... he's just so heavy."

He lifted the dog with ease and rushed toward the clinic doors.

"What happened to him?" Holly asked as she held the main door open.

"He escaped the fenced yard and ran into oncoming traffic," the woman explained.

Quentin could feel the dog's life force fading even as he settled Bear on the exam table. If Summer and Holly could save him, it would be a miracle of the Goddess.

The little girl stood off to one side as Summer and Holly examined the girl's pet. Working on instinct, he picked the child up and approached Bear's head.

"Tell him you love him and ask him to stay."

"I love you, Bear," she sobbed into the black fur. "Please don't leave me. *Please.* I love you."

Quentin set her on the floor and urged her toward the waiting room. "Now go with your mom. Doctor Summer and Miss Holly are going to fix Bear right up." After he witnessed her fling herself into her mother's embrace, Quentin shut the door. "We're going to give him a magical transfusion."

Holly gasped. "Quentin, you can't—"

"I can, and I will."

"He's lost too much blood, and I fear his internal injuries are too severe," Summer argued.

"First we start the blood draw. While that's taking place, we'll work up a spell," Quentin stated. "Between the magic in my blood and your healing abilities, we can save him."

If asked, he couldn't say why he was desperate to save this particular dog. Perhaps it was because he couldn't bear to disappoint another person in his life—*even if that person was a complete stranger.*

"He'll likely have an adverse reaction to your blood, Quentin. Different species and all," Summer warned.

"He's dead anyway. What do we have to lose?"

Holly cast a protection circle to perform the magic. Then she prepared the dog for the infusion as Summer inserted the needle into Quentin's arm where he sat outside the ring. "Sure you want to do this?"

"Yeah."

"Okay, then."

The sisters took their places, one on either side of the table where Bear rested. They clasped hands, and each placed a palm on the canine's abdomen.

"Goddess, hear our plea. Assist us in our time of need."

The candles within the ring flickered to and fro, a clear indication the spirit of the Goddess was among them. Summer locked eyes with Holly and nodded. "We need to visualize his internal organs as they would be in full health. Look at the diagram in the book. Imagine everything in working order and the blood pumping properly through his veins. Can you do that, sister?"

Holly gave an affirmative nod.

"Good. Push a white healing energy out through your palm where it is resting on his belly. I'm going to knit the tendons, tissues, blood vessels, veins, and so on. Whatever you do, don't stop feeding the healing light until I say."

"Got it."

They worked for nearly a half hour, and finally, when Quentin had nothing left to give, the women concluded their spell and closed the circle. The dog wasn't out of the woods completely, but neither was death imminent.

Quentin sat back in one of the padded chairs and closed his eyes, as weak as a newborn kitten. Summer left to notify Bear's family that it would be a wait-and-see game but that the prognosis was good.

The scent of fresh lemons teased his nostrils. A soft, warm palm settled on his cheek while another smoothed back his sweat-drenched hair.

"Quentin."

The effort to open his eyes cost him what remaining energy he had left.

"I'm going to transport you to my home in order to look after you for a while," Holly said. "You okay with that?"

"Yeah. But no taking advantage of my body in its weakened state."

"I'll try to resist the urge," she said dryly. "Hold on tight."

"I've never let go, love," he murmured before he passed out.

HOLLY LAID a cool cloth on Quentin's brow and sighed.

What he did today reminded her of all the kind gestures she'd witnessed him perform in the past. While he may be the biggest man-whore on the planet, he had a heart of gold and was ready to take on a lost cause without a moment's thought.

Because he was sleeping, she allowed herself to study his breathtaking face. She'd never seen a man as beautiful in her entire life. Not movie stars, not male models, not anyone. Quentin was a work of art. When the Goddess created him, she must've celebrated for days.

Added to his strong forehead and straight aquiline nose were his high cheekbones. That combination, along with the dark arched brows framing his warm chocolate bedroom eyes, was sheer poetry. He also had a wide smiling mouth that boasted brilliant white teeth, all in perfect alignment. There wasn't a soul on the planet who came anywhere close to matching his handsomeness.

His mouth fell open slightly as he slept.

Holly's eyes fell to his full, generous lips. The desire to kiss him was never far from the surface. Whatever their problems had been, sex wasn't one of them. Her breathing kicked up a notch, and her fingers twitched to trace his chiseled jaw. She closed her eyes and sighed a second time. Yes, she still desired him even after all they'd been through.

A sixth sense told her that she was being watched. When she opened her eyes, she sucked in her breath. Quentin's stare was hot. Bold hunger shone brightly in his gaze. The skin over her entire body tightened.

"How long have I been out?"

His deep, husky tone reached right in and tickled her lady bits.

She licked her lips and swallowed before answering. "Not too long. Maybe three hours."

They stared, lost in one another.

"Thank you for taking care of me," he said, his voice low and intimate.

"If I left you helpless in one of the exam rooms, the female staff would've been fighting each other for a chance to touch you."

He grinned and shifted the hand resting across his chest to cup her hip. The gesture was a familiar one from long ago. "In that case, I owe you doubly so."

Irritated with herself for being sucked back in, if only for a few hours, she removed his hand and snapped, "Don't act like you don't love women fighting over you."

Something akin to disappointment clouded his eyes before he closed them.

"Yep. You have me all figured out." He scrubbed his hands over his face and handed her the damp washcloth from his forehead. "Give me a few more minutes to get my legs under me, and I'll be out of your hair."

Ashamed of her churlish behavior, she cleared her throat. "You don't have to leave right away. Take your time to recover."

He snorted his disbelief and sat up. "Don't act like you give a shit now, Holly. You might shock my system into a fatal heart attack."

"I'm not a complete bitch." A forceful sneeze accompanied her statement. Before she could fist her hand to stem the avian inundation, pecking started on the bay window beside the sofa. "Oh, for fu—"

Quentin's large palm covered her mouth and cut off her colorful curse. "Not unless you want a scene from one of Hitchcock's movies."

Holly glared her frustration.

For a mere second, his eyes warmed with humor before he banked his amusement and released her. "You're not a bitch. A bit of a hellcat, but not a bitch."

He leaned his head back on the couch and stared at her through his thick black lashes. With his legs spread wide, he was the very image of sexy. Even ill, his pull was strong. Everything inside her wanted to merge and mate with him.

"You shouldn't look at me that way, love. It sends mixed signals."

"I'm not looking at you in any way, Quentin," she denied hotly.

"Mmhmm." Again, he closed his eyes.

Concern for him overpowered her pique, and she rested a hand on his thigh. "Are you sure you're okay? I think you should lie back down."

He didn't answer, and Holly knew Quentin had passed out again.

Because she'd never seen him this weak, her nerves got the better of her. She found her phone and dialed her aunt, GiGi, for assistance.

In less than five minutes, her aunt had arrived.

"What did the fool boy do?" GiGi asked.

"A blood transfusion for a Rottweiler. He was trying to save the dog's life for a little girl." And didn't that melt her heart?

GiGi glanced up sharply. "What a lovely, yet completely foolish thing to do!"

"Yes." Holly's heartfelt sigh came from the teenage girl who once loved a wild teenage boy.

"Did he do it to impress you?"

As she stared down at Quentin's incredible face, she slowly shook her head. "No. It's just who he is. Reckless. Impulsive. Sweet as the day is long."

"Sounds like you love him, child."

The statement shook her from her dreamy state. She scowled. "No. I thought I loved who he once appeared to be. I was wrong."

"That seems to be the theme of this family," GiGi chuckled. "But it also seems that perhaps the women are a bunch of blind fools. Shall I include you in the lot?"

Irritated at being lumped in with her sisters and their past relationship woes, Holly snapped, "I'll go make you tea. Let me know if you need help with him."

CHAPTER 3

"You can open your eyes, dear boy. She's gone." Quentin cracked one eye to peek from beneath his lashes before sitting up straight. "She's a hard nut to crack. You'll wear yourself out trying to convince her she's in the wrong, Miss GiGi."

"And you? Seems you've been chasing her for quite a long time. Aren't you worn out yet?"

He met her knowing violet-blue eyes and grimaced. "There are days I feel like I'm close to wearing her down. Others make me feel like I should walk away for good."

"Why don't you tell her the truth?"

Staring off in the direction Holly had gone, Quentin shrugged morosely. "If she didn't believe me then, she won't believe me now. It doesn't matter. I'll be here for her until she's safe."

"Does she at least know you aren't on my brother's payroll?"

He snorted. "You'd think she'd have figured that out a long time ago. Alastair thinks I'm incompetent and not good enough for his precious daughter. He certainly wouldn't hire me as a bodyguard for her."

"She's blind for the trees. But you're wrong about my brother. He wouldn't let you near her if he believed you incompetent." GiGi felt his pulse and did a quick check of his pupils. "Nothing wrong with you that a little rest won't cure, dear. Shall we make up an excuse to let you continue to stay close?"

"If I wasn't already in love with my prickly pear, I'd marry you in a minute, Miss GiGi." His appreciative grin couldn't be contained. In GiGi, he'd found a brilliant co-conspirator.

"Pfft. Perhaps my niece is correct. You *are* the world's biggest ladies' man."

"Can I help it if I love beautiful women?"

The timing for his statement was unfortunate since Holly chose that moment to return. Her concerned expression turned icy, and Quentin heaved an internal sigh. He couldn't win where she was concerned. It had never been more apparent than recently. The time was almost upon them for him to move on. When he did, he'd leave his heart with her forever.

When a hand patted his shoulder, he jumped. In the short time since Holly had entered the room, he'd forgotten anyone else existed.

"You should remain here for a least another few days, my boy. What you did was a serious drain on your system," GiGi said with a secretive wink only he was privy to. She faced Holly. "I'm assuming it isn't a problem for you to help care for him. He'll need twenty-four-hour care for at least three days."

"Aunt GiGi! I can't take care of him twenty-four-seven. I have a job and things I need to do."

"Well, I suppose we could always hire a nurse for him," GiGi said. "I know just the woman." She pulled her phone from her purse and scrolled through the listings. To Quentin, she said, "I think you'll like her. She's young, gorgeous, and—"

"He doesn't need a full-time nurse," Holly growled as she snatched her aunt's phone from her hand. "I'll take care of him."

"I'm sure Sophie wouldn't mind, dear. Since she's given up modeling, she's been looking for—"

"I said I'll take care of him," Holly nearly shouted.

Quentin focused on the ceiling and bit the inside of his lip. If he made eye contact with GiGi, he was sure to laugh.

"That's good, child. Perhaps while he's recovering, you can both discuss finding the last of the artifacts for your mother's recovery."

"You're on board with this now? Since when?" Holly demanded.

Quentin remained quiet to gauge GiGi's response. Holly's question was legit. Prior to this moment, GiGi had been against the scheme to collect the four ancient artifacts needed to restore Aurora Fennell-Thorne's life.

"You're all determined on this crazy course of action. I can only hope you will take this dear boy with you when you go after the scroll. He's quite the bodyguard, don't you think?"

"He's eye candy for desperate women," Holly retorted as she gathered up the washcloth and bowl of water she'd used earlier. "But whatever. For now, all I need to know is if he requires any medication for his recovery."

As GiGi fished around in her bag of tricks, he studied her. At nearly seventy-years-old, she looked incredible. With the body of a female less than half her age and not a single line on her face, she could've easily been mistaken for a woman in her early thirties. Such was the case with most witches. The cellular aging slowed to a crawl. The Thornes were luckier than most with their eye-catching beauty. He could only hope he aged half as well as the members of the Thorne family. GiGi's estranged husband, Ryker, was an idiot for not storming the proverbial castle gates and reclaiming his bride. Holly's aunt was exceptional in every way.

GiGi came up with a small box of Altoids mints and hastily ran her thumb over the tin. When he saw the design morph into one resembling a medical remedy, he almost lost it. GiGi Thorne-Gillespie was a crafty old broad, and he was quickly coming to adore her.

Once again, she faced Holly to hand over the tin. "Give him one of these every three hours as needed. Don't overdo, or you could cause stomach upset." She snapped the closure on her black bag. "I'll be back in two days to check on his progress."

Quentin captured her hand and brought it to his lips. "Thank you, Miss GiGi. You're an angel in disguise."

A slight blush crept into her cheeks. "And you, dear boy, are the devil in disguise. But oh, what a handsome charmer you are. I hope the medication helps." With a twinkle in her eye, she kissed his forehead and whispered, "Don't give up on our girl."

In the blink of an eye, the older woman teleported away, leaving Quentin and Holly alone with a wealth of silence between them.

HOLLY STARED at the tin of "medication" in her hand. She wasn't naive. She knew very well the trick her aunt had pulled with the mints. First, her nose wasn't broken. The smell of the Altoids was overwhelming. Secondly, GiGi had pulled a similar trick when Holly was a small child and didn't want to face punishment for whatever she'd done.

With a slight shake of her head, she handed the tin to Quentin. "Take them or not. At the very least, they'll give you fresh breath."

His bark of laughter nearly triggered hers in turn. Quentin had a wonderful laugh; full-bodied, deep, and contagious.

"She's one in a million. What was it like growing up with her?"

By the time Quentin had come into the picture, her aunt had been long gone. His question was curious and forthright, and Holly answered in the same honest spirit in which he'd asked. "Aunt GiGi was only around until my mother came into my life. But when Mom went into stasis, I still didn't see much of my aunt. She had a falling out with my father. I'm not sure why, but I assumed it had to do with Uncle Ryker."

"I'm sorry." Her surprise must've shown because he said, "You missed having a stable adult for the most important years of your life. It had to be difficult, considering what we are."

"You know, no one has ever understood that before," she said softly. Quentin might be the world's greatest flirt, but he was also extremely perceptive. Which might also be why he was successful with members of the opposite sex, now that she thought about it more.

"You'd be surprised what I notice about you, Holly."

The seriousness of his tone reached in and squeezed her heart. Once upon a time, she'd have taken those words at face value. She'd have hugged him and offered up a kiss to show her appreciation of his understanding. The loss stung. He had been essential to her existence—*until the day he'd broken her heart.*

Because she needed to escape his presence, she grasped the first excuse she could think of. "I was going to make lunch. Are you hungry?"

"Extremely," he murmured.

Holly swallowed hard. They both knew he wasn't referring to food. "Great," she burst out, her tone overly bright. "I'll whip us up a bite to eat."

Wry humor curled his lip. Her gaze dropped to his mouth, and heat unfurled low in her belly. What the hell was wrong with her today? First, she'd ogled his ass as he unloaded the pallet of dog food. Then, because she couldn't *not* touch him, she'd bathed his face and neck while he was sleeping. Now, she was fawning over every sideways glance.

She turned on her heel but didn't make it a single step before he'd captured her hand and tugged her into his lap. Without a by-your-leave, he kissed her; hungrily and all-consuming.

Her hands flew to his chest, whether to balance herself or to feel his large, muscled pecs was up for question. Holly didn't try to offer a token of resistance; she didn't want to. Instead, she went with the kiss. It had been too long since she'd had intimate human contact. Too long. And deep down, she missed what she'd shared with Quentin.

His kisses—deep, hot, slow, yet with enough fire to singe—drugged her mind and set her body alight. She wasn't sure how it happened, but her shirt was off, and Quentin stopped, hyper-focused on a jagged scar that ran from her collarbone to beneath her bra on the right side of her chest.

His rage was palpable.

"I should have found a way to kill him slower."

Holly gasped and scrambled backwards off Quentin's lap, crashing into the sharp corner of the coffee table. She winced and grabbed for her scrub top.

Before she could pull it over her head, he yanked it from her hand and tossed it Goddess knew where. She focused her wary gaze from his enraged face. A whisper of a memory teased the corners of her brain. "Y-you? You w-were there?"

His mouth twisted in an ugly grimace, and he looked away.

Holly surged forward, any embarrassment about her scarred body gone. She grabbed his face between her palms. "Quentin? You were there?"

A sharp, rough nod was her answer.

"How?"

"It's ancient history, love."

She ignored his gruffness. Quentin always became irritable when he didn't want to answer a question.

"How?" she demanded.

"Holly, please don't ask me about that night." His dark, tortured eyes lifted to meet her probing gaze.

"I need to know. All this time, I thought it was my father who saved me from Beau and Michelle. But it was you, wasn't it?"

Quentin closed his eyes and nodded. "Yes."

The memory of the night her husband and her best friend had tried to kill her came rushing back. Holly was transported back in time through the brutal memories.

Beau had picked her up from the diner where she was waitressing that night. Coincidentally, Quentin had been loitering around inside over a cup of coffee. As she distributed tickets to the last of her customers—Quentin included—he had clasped her hand and lightly squeezed down.

"Don't go with him, Holly."

The deep frown on his face, his tone of voice, and the fact that he'd used her real name in place of a pet name had halted her in her tracks.

Despite his betrayal, she sensed that in this, he did have her best interests at heart. She lowered her voice and cast a quick look toward Beau who stood impatiently by the exit. "What do you know?"

"Nothing concrete. A feeling at best. I…" Quentin shook his head and gave her wrist a light squeeze. "Stay with me."

There was a desperate quality underlying Quentin's words, and Holly almost caved. His unease fed hers. She'd been restless all day, and this discussion only made it worse.

"Holly! Come on! We're going to be late," Beau called from the door with a glare in their direction.

She shifted her attention between the two men and noted the animosity. It had been there since she'd started dating Beau and hadn't ended with her marriage. Quentin hated Beau with every fiber of his being. He'd gone on to say as much.

"Holly." The urgency in Quentin's voice struck a chord in her chest. "Don't go with him."

"I have to," she whispered. "He's my husband."

"Say the word, and I'll take you away."

Beau stalked to the booth. In an aggressive move, her husband grabbed her arm, causing Holly to wince in pain.

Beau's roughness was all it took for Quentin to snap. He surged to his feet and ripped Beau's hand from her. At six foot six with a chest almost one and a half times wider than the average male, Quentin's height and build were imposing. In a rage, as he was now, he resembled an avenging angel.

"Touch her like that again, and I will rip your arms from their sockets," he growled.

"She's *my* wife," Beau snarled.

Holly wedged herself between the two men and placed a hand over Quentin's heart. The wild, fast-paced rhythm was at direct odds with the calm mask he'd donned the second she touched him.

Their gazes connected. His was as dark as she'd ever seen. She tried to bank the worry in her own.

"It's okay, Quentin. Thank you for caring, but Beau wouldn't hurt me."

Quentin's brows dipped together, and a troubled light entered his eyes. "Call me if you need me."

"Of course." But she never would. There was too much hurt and too many hard feelings between them. He had let her leave with Beau. *The second worst mistake of her life.*

Unbeknownst to Holly at the time, Beau and Michelle had been having an affair. That night, the two of them decided to put into action their plan to do away with the woman standing in their way. Mostly because they were the only two non-magical humans who knew what she was, and they feared her. Feared what she might do if they were found out—or at least that's what Michelle had later confessed. That Beau stood to inherit Holly's multi-million-dollar trust fund probably weighed heavily into their actions as well.

Beau had taken her to an out-of-the-way location where Michelle was already waiting. Holly never saw his long hunting knife until it slashed through the flesh and muscle of her chest.

As she stared in shocked horror, her mind registered the pain and her lungs struggled in their effort to draw a breath. Her eyes rolled back in her head, and blackness descended. Her one final thought had been that she should have listened to Quentin and the little voice that had been straining to be heard in the back of her mind.

Later, after all was said and done, she'd sworn she heard screams and smelled the scent of burning flesh. Arms had cradled her, and droplets of an unknown liquid had warmed her chilled skin.

Now, seven years after the attack, a new memory surfaced.

"Don't leave me, love. You hang on! You understand? You'd better hang on, Holly!"

Quentin's voice. How had she forgotten?

She gazed up at him in wide-eyed wonder. "I can't believe you were there. How did you know?"

A flash of unnamed emotion flitted across his face. If Holly didn't know better, she'd suspect he was uncomfortable with the conversation. Unsure why, she remained silent, allowing him to continue.

"I couldn't shake the feeling." He traced the shape of her scar. "As you walked out the door of the diner, it grew exponentially. I…" He paused, and his troubled eyes rose to lock with hers. "I felt like a damned stalker, but I cloaked myself and my bike, then followed. If you were okay, I intended to leave, but the stabbing happened almost immediately."

There was an element of truth Quentin was holding back. She sensed it more than anything else, but she allowed him his secrets. Without his interference, she'd have been in a morgue.

"Did I imagine you holding me afterwards?" she asked quietly.

"No, you didn't imagine it." He ran a hand through his long, thick mane. "Christ, Hol, it was the worst night of my life. I thought you were lost to me for good. I wasn't sure my healing energy could save you. Your lung was punctured… all that blood…" He exhaled a shaky breath. "I used your phone to call your dad. He arrived and healed you. Then he sent me away." The haunted look in his eyes grew stronger. "He told me it was for the best. That if it ever came to light I was there that night, it might hurt the prosecution's case against Michelle. He feared it might look like a warped love triangle."

"But why didn't you tell me? Why let me believe all these years that it was my father who saved me?"

Quentin didn't answer. Once again, his gaze fell to the scar. "Why didn't you have it removed? GiGi or your father could have easily done it at any point."

She dropped her gaze and shrugged. "I wanted a reminder of that night."

"For the love of the Goddess, why?"

"To remind me of my stupidity in trusting men."

Quentin's face became a cool mask, and he settled back against the edge of the sofa. "I see."

"Do you?" Her anger came from nowhere and coursed through her veins. It throbbed and pounded against the walls of her brain with the rapid beat of her heart. "Because I don't! I don't know what it is about me that makes men cheat, or what it is about me that makes me unlovable."

His strong arms gathered her close. It became imperative that she fight his hold. She didn't dare soften.

"Let me go!" She struggled against his embrace.

"No, love. Not until you listen to me. And I'm only going to say this once more. I want you to finally hear what I'm telling you." He gripped her chin and forced her to look at him. "I love you, Holly."

"No!"

"Yes, dammit!" He gave her a gentle shake. "I always have."

"Then why did you cheat on me?" she cried out. The question had been ruthlessly suppressed since the night the incident happened.

"I never did." The sincerity on his face and in his heart couldn't be mistaken. She shook her head in denial. If he hadn't cheated, then Holly had been the worst sort of fool for believing Michelle.

Quentin nodded the moment Holly registered her mistake.

"She was your friend. It made sense that you would believe her. But after..." He shook his head. "After what they did, I thought surely you'd understand and recognize her scheming for what it was."

The agony in his voice broke her.

"Ohmygod, Quentin!" She sobbed his name. "Ohmygod!"

"The worst part was that you forgave her and allowed her back into your life after we had supposedly slept together. But you wouldn't forgive me. It never even happened, Hol, and yet, you kept me at arm's length. I thought I would lose my mind."

Holly wrapped her arms around his neck and clung to him for all she was worth. What a complete sucker she'd been! Why had it never occurred to her to question Michelle?

"I'm sorry, Quentin. I'm so sorry."

The air around them shifted, and a crack rent the space to Holly's right.

"I wondered if you two would ever patch up your differences. I'm glad you finally have."

Holly stared in disbelief at her father. "Were you spying on us?"

Indignation colored Alastair Thorne's aristocratic features. In an arrogant voice that never failed to irritate Holly, he said, "Your lack of faith in me is astounding."

"What makes you believe we patched things up?"

One brow arched. "Perhaps it's the way you are wrapped around the man, like a vine clinging to a tree."

Holly quickly disentangled herself.

"Or perhaps you scried right before you arrived," Quentin offered up in a dry, amused tone.

"Perhaps," Alastair agreed. "Don't worry. I didn't see anything compromising."

Holly snapped her fingers to conjure herself a new top. She waited until she was covered before she asked, "What do you want, Alastair?"

"Quentin's help for the final piece to revive your mother."

CHAPTER 4

"*N*o! Absolutely not!" Holly said for the fourth time since they'd started their discussion. She stood between the two men, arms crossed and foot tapping. "There is no way Quentin is putting himself in danger on our behalf."

"Isn't it cute that she thinks she has a say?" murmured Quentin.

On the coffee table was a glass of water she'd brought for him earlier. From the corner of his eye, he noticed the bubbles start to form. Yes, Holly was in high form. She whirled on him, and he couldn't stop his besotted grin. She was beautiful in her fierceness.

"I damned well *do* have a say," she seethed before she sneezed.

Both men clenched a hand into a fist and sent out a pulse of energy to magically stave off the impending bird attack. Quentin met Alastair's amused gaze. It felt like the two of them had always been at odds, but the one thing each understood and respected about the other was their unspoken desire to always protect Holly, no matter the cost.

Quentin turned his attention back to the toe-tapping termagant. "I'll do whatever is necessary to keep you safe, love. You should know that by now. And part of that is going after the scroll your father needs to bring your mother out of stasis."

"Then we'll go together," she insisted.

"No, we won't. There's no need for you to do anything of the sort. Zhu Lin is gone. It's safe for me to go alone. I don't need the badass Thornes to take charge."

Bringing up Lin's name made him uneasy. Sure, the bastard was dead, but Quentin still shuddered when he thought of what Holly's poor sister Spring had gone through at the hands of the drug lord she'd been sold to by that evil fuck.

Spring Thorne had been unable to recover her memory on her own after the Goddess Isis had revived her. She'd needed a magical assist from the Goddess herself. Despite her ability to see the past, Spring could only view her pre-abduction life in a detached manner with no feelings one way or the other, because to her new self, she hadn't really lived it.

He was grateful Spring had driven the Karma bus over Zhu Lin's psycho ass the day she buried him alive. Quentin would lose his mind if anything of that nature happened to Holly.

Holly moved to stand toe-to-toe with him and slapped a hand on his chest. "If Lin is gone, there is no need for *me* not to go by myself, is there?"

Alastair gently cleared his throat and addressed Holly. "There is another who has taken Lin's place as head of the Désorcelers society. Victor Salinger. He's dangerous and wily in a way Lin never was. It's safer if you remain off his radar, child."

"No way am I letting Quentin do this alone. What if something happens to him? How am I supposed to live with that?"

A warmth similar to hope spread through him, and he captured her hand in his. "Are you finally admitting you love me, my prickly pear?"

Tears gathered in her troubled turquoise eyes and lent a heart-breaking quality to her already desolate expression. "I don't want anything to happen to you."

"If I know you'll be waiting, I'll move heaven and earth to come back to you," he promised.

She swallowed hard and closed her eyes.

Quentin sighed. Once again, she'd effectively shut him out. She had never budged an inch or admitted she might care for him in all this time. *Nor would she.*

Because he had to comfort her as well as himself, he tucked her against his chest and rested his cheek on the top of her glossy, dark hair. "You don't have to say it, Hol. It's okay."

On Holly's wedding day, the morning before she and Beau had declared their vows, he'd tried one last time to sway her. She'd claimed she loved Beau and insisted Quentin leave her be.

To this day, the memory of their confrontation made him achy and raw. It had also damaged a fundamental part of his soul when she said she didn't love him in return. As far as the Thorne family legend went, Thornes only loved once. Which meant, if Holly had truly loved Beau, she'd never love Quentin—no matter how much he wished it.

All the fun, playful banter on his part was an act. One he could no longer maintain. But he could do this last thing for her before he moved on. In the doing, he'd try to make sure her family's enemies were removed from the playing field and no longer posed a threat. Holly would be allowed to live out her life in a safe, carefree manner.

He met Alastair's watchful gaze. Another silent understanding passed between the two men. Quentin suspected Alastair knew how much he loved Holly but that he was also at the end of his rope. He could no longer continue to be in her presence without her returning his affections.

"I'm going after the scroll, Holly," he told her quietly, careful to use her given name. The time had come to start the distancing process, and the best way to go about that was to dispose of the familiarity they'd always shared. "Consider it my last gift to you."

Her head came up and knocked him in the chin. It didn't surprise him when she didn't wince. The woman was as hardheaded as they came. She had to be to continue to love a man who had tried to murder her. Why else keep the loser's last name? Beau was dead, killed by Quentin's own hand. But she continued to use the last name of Hill in memory of that asshat.

"What do you mean by last gift?" Her voice was harsh with a hint of shrill, and both men cringed at the sound.

Quentin refused to answer. What would be the point of another argument?

"I think the poor boy is positively peckish from lack of nutrition, child," Alastair said as he stepped forward. "Why not make him a bite to eat?"

"If he's hungry, he can conjure food, *father*."

Quentin did the one thing that he knew would drive her away. "When are you going to get past the pettiness and grow up, Holly? He's not the enemy."

Her eyes flew wide, and her mouth rounded in a perfect O. In their entire relationship, he'd never spoken to her in such a manner. Sure, he'd been angry, and they had volleyed heated words, but he'd never criticized her, and especially not in front of Alastair. Partly, because Quentin feared Holly's father would obliterate him on the spot for his disrespect, but mostly because he knew Holly didn't take any type of criticism well.

Her gasp of shock meant he'd struck a nerve.

Holly recovered enough to mask her features. She lifted her chin. "You're right. I'm sorry. It's obvious you two want to talk. I'll head back to the clinic and leave you to it." Before she teleported, she met Quentin's eyes one last time. "Please don't leave before I've had a chance to say goodbye."

He nodded but made no promise. A long, drawn-out goodbye wasn't for him. There really was no point. He'd be gone for good by the time she returned.

After Holly left, Alastair bent to retrieve her discarded scrub top. As Quentin watched, the other man turned it right-side out, folded it, and placed it on the chair seat. What struck him as odd was how Alastair smoothed out the wrinkles in a seemingly loving manner where the garment lay folded.

"You know, the fact that you love your daughter is obvious to everyone but her. She's never confided why she holds such animosity toward you. At least, not to me. Maybe because your argument happened after she and I broke up. Care to share?"

Alastair continued to stare at the top. "Holly believes I betrayed her trust and was responsible for her mother's injury."

"Were you? Responsible, that is?"

His question caught Alastair off guard. The other man's deep frown said as much. "I suppose so. I hadn't anticipated Rorie following me that day, but I should have. When Lin pulled a gun on me, she threw herself in the path of the bullet. Lin used to lace his ammunition with a poison mixture fatal to witches. And while I rushed her to my sister, GiGi, as quickly as I could, it wasn't fast enough. Rorie has languished in stasis while we try to come up with another way to bring her back."

"No matter where a bullet hit you, the wound was fatal?"

"Yes. And now Salinger has adopted the practice of using laced bullets. Or his mercenaries have anyway. There *is* an antidote if given immediately, but the plant it comes from is nearly extinct. Isis gifted us a plant to treat Autumn when she fell ill due to the poison. The last I heard, Spring was trying to repopulate the species, but that takes time even for witches."

"What you are saying is that I'm screwed should I get shot by him or his army while retrieving this scroll," Quentin said wryly.

"I'm saying don't get shot, son. It would be one more thing my daughter would hate me for."

"What else happened between you, Mr. Thorne? It can't only be about her mother. Aurora was in stasis when I was dating Holly. She may have acted out, but she didn't truly hate you then."

Alastair's mouth twisted in a semblance of a bittersweet smile. "Aren't you the perceptive one?"

"I try."

With a tug of his shirt cuffs, Alastair launched into an explanation. "I didn't approve of that waste-of-space Beau Hill. I tried to get Holly to see reason, and she refused. Being the brilliant strategist I am..." Here Alastair rolled his eyes. "... I told her if she married him, I intended to cut her off financially. She couldn't see it, but he was always out for the family money."

"Ouch."

"Indeed." Alastair shook his perfectly styled, blond head. "She told me she didn't want one red cent from me, then she got a job at that godforsaken diner in town."

"I tried to purchase the diner once."

Alastair's brows rose in sharp, silent question.

"I wanted to make sure she always had a job if she needed one." Quentin chuckled softly and shook his head. "Imagine my surprise when your name was on the deed. If I had to guess, it was so you could pay her a healthy wage, regardless of the fact that she disobeyed you and married that prick."

"Perhaps." Alastair gave a suave one-shouldered shrug. "I never thanked you properly for your part in saving her life." He walked to him and held out his hand. "Thank you, son."

"And I never thanked you for sparing my life the night Holly and I were arrested down by the airstrip," Quentin countered as he accepted Alastair's hand. "Thank you, sir."

"You're a good man. Holly can do—and has done—a lot worse."

All humor left Quentin. "She loved him. I don't know why, but she did. I suppose that's the reason for her shitty choices."

"She didn't love him, boy. She loves you. Always has. Why would you think otherwise?"

Disbelief warred with incredulousness that Alastair misread the situation. The guy *never* misread anything. "She told me on her wedding day."

"Ah. Yes, well, if I had to guess, Holly was trying to save face."

"Save face for what?"

"Your affair with the gorgeous, deceitful Michelle."

Rage exploded in Quentin's brain like an undetected aneurysm. "I never had a goddamned affair with her!"

Alastair held up his hands. "I know, son. If you had, you wouldn't be within twenty feet of my daughter."

Somewhat mollified, Quentin nodded, sat, and rested his head in his hands. "Can we move to a different subject now? I'm tired of rehashing the past. It changes nothing."

"Certainly."

ALASTAIR STUDIED Quentin where he sat on the couch. The young man looked world-weary and torn. It wasn't surprising. Holly had led him on a merry chase, and the poor fellow was exhausted from the runaround.

"The scroll is in a vault in Greece."

"Tell me what I need to know, and I'll go today."

"You have no intention of sticking around to say goodbye to my daughter, do you?"

"No. I'll get the scroll, and then I'm gone. I won't be where I'm not wanted. Not anymore. But if I can neutralize Salinger's threat, I will."

Alastair ambled around the living room, touching an item here or there. His curiosity was caught by the group of photos on the wall beside the front door. One held his attention more than the others. It was a small black-and-white image of himself holding Holly as a toddler. He was gazing down at her with amused affection as she pointed over his shoulder. GiGi had taken that shot. In it, she'd caught all the love he'd felt for his precious baby girl.

"I'm surprised she has that on her wall," Quentin said from his place on the couch.

Alastair ran a finger across the cool surface of the glass. "Yes."

"As much as she claims to hate you, she has a photo of you on her wall. Telling, no?"

"I suppose it is," he agreed. He scanned the rest of the grouping, noting none of Quentin and Holly. To his mind, that was far more revealing.

As if Quentin sensed Alastair's thoughts, he said, "It's also telling there are none of the ones Holly was always snapping of us together."

"Perhaps it hurts her more to see the two of you together."

"Right." Quentin let out a harsh laugh. "What are the coordinates of the vault?"

"It isn't that simple." He returned and settled on the arm of the chair across from the younger man. "The vault is located in the National Archaeological Museum in Athens."

"It's a simple matter of cloaking myself before closing time, slipping into the vault, finding the scroll, and teleporting out."

"Except the museum belongs to the Witches' Council. There are wards and spells to prevent that from happening."

"Of *course* there are," Quentin groaned in disgust. "What's your retrieval idea?"

"I want you to seduce Selene Barringer. She's the head of acquisitions for the Council in Europe."

"Similar to what your son, Nash, does here?"

"Yes."

"Fine. Then give me an extra day to regain my strength." Quentin's dull-eyed stare focused on him. "Meet me in the diner tomorrow morning at ten with the information on this Selene chick. I assume you have a detailed file?"

He nodded.

"I'll do whatever is necessary."

"If you seduce her, you'll be saying goodbye to whatever chance you have with Holly."

"That should make you happy. You never approved of me anyway."

"You were wild in those days."

Quentin laughed long and loud. "No, sir. Your daughter was wild in those days. I was just along for the ride because how could I not? She was magnificent." He sobered and stared at the ground. "Still is."

"If you love her, why leave?"

"The whipped dog routine is getting old, Mr. Thorne. It's past time I got a life, don't you think?"

"Where will you go?"

"Why do you care?" Quentin asked harshly. "Seriously? Why?"

"I find I like you, son."

"That's sure to set Holly against me if she ever finds out." Quentin stood and met his gaze. "Maybe you should let her know. It will help in the long run. Final nail in the coffin and all that." He straightened the pillows on the couch and folded the blanket over the back, effectively removing any trace he'd been there. "I'll see you tomorrow, sir."

CHAPTER 5

"*W*hat's wrong with you? Are you okay?"

Holly lifted her head from the blank computer screen she'd been staring at for the last three minutes. Her twin sister sat perched on the edge of the reception desk, blonde and beautiful with a sunny expression on her face. One foot swinging back and forth to a rhythm only she heard. It was disturbing that she never sensed Summer before she spoke. The lack of attention to her surroundings proved how deeply engrossed Holly had been in her own problems.

"I'm fine."

Summer reached forward and flicked Holly's earlobe.

"Ouch!"

"It's what you get for being a dirty liar. Now, tell me what's really wrong? Is Quentin okay from earlier today? No complications from the blood draw?"

"Quentin's fine," Holly ground out.

"That sounded convincing. What did he do to piss you off this time?"

A flutter of irritation swept through her. Why did everyone always assume she was pissed at Quentin? Granted, she didn't fawn all over him like other women did with their guys, but she didn't hate him. Not anymore. Maybe not ever. "Nothing. I'm worried about him, if you must know."

Summer straightened and stared down at her, all teasing gone. "What's going on?"

"I think he intends to find the scroll and then take off."

"Surely he wouldn't take off with the last item we need to revive our Mother."

"No. I mean he intends to retrieve it for *us*, then leave for good. *I think*." She rested her forehead in her palms. It was too damned much to pretend she wasn't bothered by his behavior. "I don't know. I can't seem to trust my own instincts." Holly raised her head and met Summer's concerned gaze. "He was the one who saved me from Beau and Michelle. Can you believe it? *Him*, not our father like I'd believed all this time."

"Are you serious? How the hell did that happen?" Summer's swearing was a testament to her shock. Even as she sneezed, she clenched her fist to ward off the mice that tended to show up when she was upset.

Holly gave her a rundown of the facts.

The twins stared at one another, each reeling from the implications of the rescue. Summer was the first to speak. "You've always believed he cheated with Michelle?" At Holly's nod, she continued. "What if he didn't? What if she really did lie, and he's hung around all this time because he loves you?"

Holly had come to the realization that her ex-bestie had indeed lied, and it made her sick at heart. Michelle had been incredibly convincing. Her ex-best friend had been such an accomplished actress that she had no idea Michelle was putting out for Holly's husband. She recalled all the times Quentin had defended himself, had tried to make her see reason. She'd always thought he was sorry he'd gotten caught to begin with. A sob caught in Holly's throat. She'd wronged Quentin on every level.

"Oh, Summer. I made such a huge mistake."

Summer grabbed her hand and dragged her to the private office in the back of the clinic. The room was occupied by Audrey, one of the veterinary assistants. "Out. And stop calling your boyfriend on company time. Have Patti man the front desk, and when I come out, I expect those kennels to be spotless."

Holly kept it together until Audrey left. But the second the door closed, the tap turned on and tears poured from her eyes like a geyser. Summer held her and rocked her like a small child.

"Shhh, it's all right, sister. Quentin understands. He wouldn't have hung around this long if he didn't."

"You didn't see. There was something different about him today. Something resigned."

"We're Thornes. Have you seen Autumn scry? He can run, but he can't hide."

Holly produced something similar to a laugh-snort-cough. It wasn't pretty, but Summer was quick with a tissue and an order to mop up everything above the shoulders.

"I have an idea." Summer opened her bottom drawer and pulled out a scrying mirror and a white candle.

"You happen to have a mirror in your desk? Honestly?"

"What are you trying to say?"

"You're as bad as Autumn."

"Oh, and it wasn't you who made popcorn or encouraged me to spy on Coop when we'd broken up?"

"Shut up and cast the spell."

Holly passed a hand over the mirror as Summer lit the candle.

"Ostendo!"

Within a minute, the sisters were eavesdropping on Alastair and Quentin's discussion about the vault in Greece.

"You have no intention of sticking around to say goodbye to my daughter, do you?"

"No. I'll get the scroll, and then I'm gone. I won't be where I'm not wanted. Not anymore. But if I can neutralize Salinger's threat, I will."

Holly reeled back in shock. Her hurt and betrayal were seasoned with a heavy dash of self-loathing. *She'd* done this. She'd finally driven him away for good.

As they continued to listen, she was certain the crack in her heart widened. Quentin had agreed to seduce another woman because he'd given up on her. Tears poured unchecked down her cheeks, and even Summer's warm, supportive hug couldn't break through the grief Holly was experiencing.

"He doesn't want me anymore," she whispered after Quentin had walked out the front door of her living room.

"No, sister. You are completely missing what he's saying." Summer smoothed the hair back from Holly's face. "He has given up hope that you might ever return his feelings. You need to nip this in the bud."

"How? What do I do?"

The air around them shifted, and her father walked through the rift in space. "You go after him, child. Trust me, Selene will eat him up and spit him out."

Holly snapped.

One second she was in control; the next, she wanted to maim him for what he'd set in motion. She flew at him, fists raised to do damage. "I hate you! You ruin everything! Always. You have to butt in where you're not wanted." The impact of her balled hands might have hurt a lesser man, but her father never uttered a word or even grunted his discomfort. "How could you?"

As suddenly as her rage surfaced, it was gone, as was her energy. She fell into a heap at his feet. "I'm so stupid."

Summer took a step forward, but their father waved her off and squatted beside Holly. "No. You *aren't* stupid. You are beautiful and open, with a heart bigger than the whole of this continent. You were betrayed by consummate liars. However, Quentin wasn't one of them."

She lifted her head and stared at him. What was he saying? He knew all along?

"I love you, Holly Anne. You are one of the three brightest stars in my universe." His voice was as raw as she'd ever heard it. Honest, too. The sincerity was there for all who cared to see. "What I did today, I did for you. Do you honestly believe I didn't know you'd spy on our conversation? Did you hear how adamant he was when he said he'd never cheated? And since the stabbing, have you never wondered why he scarcely left your side?" He released a heart-heavy sigh and grabbed her hand. "You have always been so damned stubborn."

Belatedly, she registered he was able to swear without sneezing. Since meeting her long-lost twin this past year, she'd come to realize if she or Summer swore while touching each other, they could stem off the sneeze that brought the birds and rodents.

A tight ball of emotion in Holly's throat prevented an answer.

"He killed for you, and he'd die for you in a second. Can you say the same? What would you sacrifice for him?"

"Everything." Her whisper was barely audible, but he heard her all the same because he nodded and handed her a slip of paper.

"He'll check in here tomorrow at six p.m. I've booked the adjoining suite for you." He looked like he wanted to say more but refrained. With an elegance that was standard for Alastair Thorne, he rose. "Goodbye, dear girl. I hope you find your heart's desire in Greece."

With a simple snap of his finger, he teleported away.

"Daddy!" she called. But he was gone. Distraught, she looked at her stunned sister and asked, "What the hell did he mean by that?" She promptly sneezed but was too scattered to remember to stave off the birds that started pecking at Summer's office window.

Summer looked as stunned as Holly felt. "If I had to guess, he exited your life."

Trepidation and anguish paralyzed her. Her father was as steady as the day was long, wasn't he? "He wouldn't."

"Yet, I think he did." Summer sat next to her and pulled her close. "When have you ever heard him say goodbye?"

"What have I done?"

Summer squeezed her once and helped her to her feet. "It doesn't matter. We're going to fix this. You go after Quentin, and when I have time, I'll see about our father. Don't waste the gift he gave you."

"Right." But still Holly was reluctant to go. She was unable to wrap her mind around all that had taken place in the last half hour. She gave voice to her most horrific fear. "What if Quentin doesn't want me anymore?"

"Didn't the Great Alastair Thorne just get done saying you weren't stupid? Don't prove him wrong now. Get your ass in gear and get ready to hightail it to Greece. And be sure to conjure a sexy outfit when you get there. Lingerie with pale pink bows on black lace drives men wild."

For the first time, Holly laughed. "You know this how?"

"Never you mind. Get going. I've got the office and sanctuary covered."

"I love you, sister."

Summer grinned. "Of course you do. I'm amazing. Now go!"

HOLLY POPPED back home on the off chance Quentin might return because, in all the years he'd been her shadow, she had never learned where he lived. She had no idea where to look for him now.

After a few hours, it became apparent he had no intention of returning. She had to face the fact that he was through. Yet she was damned if she'd let him walk away now. Not after discovering he'd saved her, never cheated, *and* still loved her. The man had to be a fool if he thought she wasn't going to lift a finger to stop him.

In her bedroom, she opened her bottom drawer and shoved aside the few old articles of clothing hiding her most treasured possession: her photo album. Holly hesitated to remove it from its nest. If she opened it, she'd also open the locked gates of her heart and allow all the old emotions to flood back in. The purple twelve-by-twelve album contained images of all those she held dear. She hadn't opened it in years other than to add a few recent photos of her new sisters to the end of the book. Most certainly never to look at the record of the early part of her life.

Now, for the first time in nine years, she started from the beginning. Family pictures, like the ones of her mother holding her while her father lovingly smiled down upon them, glared back at her as if to say "Where have you been? How could you reject us?" But those photographs, along with the ones she knew she'd see of her and Quentin on the coming pages, were like a dagger to her heart. It had been better to shove those old memories away and never dust them off. Otherwise, she'd dwell in the past, and Holly had needed to continue to move forward for her own sanity.

Her father had once encouraged her to seek therapy. But as she sat across from the counselor, she had found it impossible to face the past. At the time, the wounds had been too fresh.

Now, as she sat cross-legged on the floor in front of her old, distressed Chesterfield dresser and thumbed through the book, her eyes filled with tears at all the love and joy she'd ignored. Her finger traced her mother's beloved face before touching her father's. Despite what everyone believed, she'd always loved her dad. However, she refused to be manipulated, and that's one thing at which Alastair Thorne excelled.

With closed eyes and a deep breath, she turned the page. When she opened them again, she knew what she'd see: Quentin's laughing face shining up at her. The bright, love-filled gaze would be only for the fun-loving young woman wielding the camera. For that carefree, naive girl who stood over him that day in the park and who pretended she was a journalist, snapping pictures of the guy with the movie-star good looks.

"Mr. Buchanan, what is the first thing you are going to do with all the millions you'll make when Hollywood comes calling?" she had teased.

"You're crazy, love. Put the camera down and come here," he'd said.

"Is that a 'no comment,' sir?"

He had shot a quick glance around and snapped his fingers. The camera flew from her hands, and he turned it on her. "We could always cloak ourselves, and I could take nude shots of you."

His suggestion sparked a fire in her lower abdomen. Quentin had a low, wicked way of speaking that tore right through her objections and made her body come to life.

In recent years, in self-preservation, Holly had erected mental pictures of him in Michelle's arms. Then, whenever he'd came on to Holly, she'd been immune to his charms. But now, she was forced to erase her false images and look at the real man. It was easier to see that he hadn't betrayed her and that *she* had betrayed *him* by not believing in him. In them.

Sucking in her breath, Holly opened her eyes. She viewed the old four-by-six photograph through misty eyes. How could she be so blind? Not now, not due to her blurry vision from her tears, but then, when it mattered and was important to see the truth? To see that Quentin would kill for her; would sacrifice his freedom when it came down to it; would head halfway around the world on a fool's errand to obtain a magical object for the benefit of *her* mother?

Yes, she needed to make it right. If she could turn back time and go back to that horrific day when she'd caught Michelle putting the moves on Quentin, she wouldn't have stormed out. She would have stayed, throat punched that vicious twatsicle, and thrown herself into Quentin's waiting embrace. Because he would've had his arms open, ready and willing to hold her as he always had.

Reflection hurt like a bitch.

"I'm sorry, Quentin. So very sorry, my love."

She pressed the open album to her chest and let the long-suppressed sobs take hold.

CHAPTER 6

Quentin sipped the black sludge the diner called coffee, as he idly watched the many passersby outside. It was symbolic that this was the booth he previously occupied on what he considered the last happy day he'd spent with Holly. In his mind, he'd always associated this table with her. Their first date, the night before her engagement, and the night she'd been stabbed—in each instance, he'd been seated here. Yeah, maybe it was fitting that he sat here now when he was finally going to exit her life. It had gone downhill from that first moment anyway.

If he closed his eyes, he could recall in great detail their initial date.

She'd been wearing a vivid teal V-neck button-down top that brought out the color of her eyes, and a pair of ass-hugging jeans that made his hands itch to touch. Her chestnut hair, lightened by coppery highlights, had been left loose about her face and shoulders. But it was her eyes, those sad, soul-destroying eyes, that had called to the orphaned boy in him. This lovely girl had known heartbreak and loneliness.

Across the table, she chattered on with an animation that lit her from within and made Quentin want to capture her unique loveliness for his own. And he had to a large degree, but Holly Thorne had been a force of nature who couldn't be contained for long.

She rambled about the day's events, none of which were important to him, but they'd mattered to her, and he listened with rapt attention. He was quick to tease her if she became too worked up over a particular topic.

The chime of a bell brought him back from the past to see Alastair Thorne stride through the diner entrance. Although he'd probably never say, Quentin admired Holly's father. The guy was self-assured and wore his power like a cloak of royalty about him. Non-magical humans wouldn't see his light, but they could understand the air of a man in charge. As such, Alastair commanded respect and a healthy dose of fear.

Quentin stood to shake hands. "Sir."

"Son."

"You look a little upset."

Surprise sent Alastair's dark blond brows skyward. "How so?"

The question was legit because Holly's father was a master at hiding his feelings. Quentin could only hope to achieve that level of perceived indifference one day.

"The tiredness in your face and the tight lines around your mouth." He shrugged. He made a study of faces to watch for enemies, his own when he was young and then for Holly after they'd hooked up. Of which, her family had plenty.

"In a word—Holly."

"Dare I ask?"

Alastair seemed to struggle with how much he wanted to say. In a rare moment, he openly shared his thoughts. "I said goodbye to her yesterday. She professed her distaste for me, and I thought to do her a solid by disappearing from her life for good."

Never mind that Alastair had said "do her a solid," which in itself was flabbergasting, the fact that he'd said goodbye to his beloved daughter left Quentin with his mouth hanging open. Recovering from the shock of these two things took a minute.

"Wow! I bet that took the wind right out of her sails." He shook his head and took a sip of his coffee. He grimaced his distaste.

"Why do you drink that swill?"

His head came up, and he pinned Alastair with a stare. "You always did when you visited Holly."

The transformation from cool indifference to vast amusement on Alastair's face was a sight to behold. "Son. I'm a warlock. Do you honestly believe I didn't change the contents of my mug?"

Quentin grunted and took another sip. He'd be damned if he'd admit to being a chump for love. He'd already been that for too many damned years to count.

"What do you have for me?"

"If you want to be free of my family, you don't have to do this. I can find another way."

"What else do I have to do with my time? It's one last hoorah before I go find a life."

"You really are ready to move on from Holly?"

"Yes." He stared down moodily into the black liquid. The dark reflection was of a morose man. "What choice do I have? Besides, you did. Maybe Holly can find happiness when the two people who annoy her the most disappear from her life." He lifted the mug. "Cheers."

Alastair slid a manila envelope across the tattered Formica surface. "Here."

"And on another note, you're richer than God. How about you fix up this dump?" He tapped the scarred table to emphasize the need.

"You are in excellent form, boy. I'm not sure I've ever borne witness to you in such a surly mood. But to answer your question, the locals like the ambiance. The chef's kitchen, however, is state-of-the-art."

Quentin shot a glance around the empty diner and then toward the snoozing Pete in the corner booth by the kitchen. "If you say so." He picked up the package.

"The envelope contains images of the museum, vault, all the key players, and a hotel reservation. Selene is intelligent, beautiful, and vicious when the need arises. Although she works for the Council, it's my belief that she is loyal to Victor Salinger. Don't underestimate her."

"Duly noted. I'll be back before the week is out." He tapped the thick envelope against his palm. "I'm assuming there is at least a description of the scroll in question?"

"There are images, and a formula to test the paper to make sure it's authentic. You'll also feel the power of the artifact, but that could be spelled. Don't take chances. Make sure it's the correct item before you get out. Also, there is a fake in that envelope to replace it. You'll need to use the incantation I've added to make it appear like the original."

Alastair straightened his tie. A sure sign he was bothered or, at the least, a bit nervous. Quentin doubted Holly's father realized he had a tell.

"Any questions?"

He could only think of one. "What did Holly say to you yesterday that you felt the need to vacate her life?"

The look on Alastair's face switched to a calm, neutral expression even as his sapphire eyes darkened to gray. Another tell. Iris changes were unique to witches. "She said she hated me and that I ruined her life."

"Jesus!" Quentin felt the impact, and he wasn't even the recipient of her anger. "That had to hurt. I'm sorry."

"You have nothing to apologize for, and neither does she. She feels how she feels. But if it makes her happier to have me gone, so be it."

For once, they sat in perfect accord. Each willing to exit Holly's life to lessen the pain of all involved.

"I'll get your scroll, Alastair. One of us deserves to be happy. I hope you are able to wake Holly's mother."

"Thank you, son. I wish you happy as well."

"On that note, I have plans to make."

"What do you intend to do when you return? I can guess, but humor me."

"Sell my home. It was designed for Holly anyway. Then, who knows? Maybe I'll like Greece and stay there. Or maybe I'll take the time and travel Europe again. It's always been a dream to live there."

"I see."

Quentin stood and threw money on the table. "It's okay, you know. None of this is on you, sir. You have to know that, right?"

"To a degree, it is." Alastair rose gracefully to his full height of six-four, a few inches short of Quentin's massive frame. "I drove her into Beau's arms."

"No. Michelle did that. You cemented her marriage to that asshole when you drew a line in the sand in your attempt to prevent her from making the biggest mistake of her life. But again, that was Holly's immature choice, not yours."

"You've always had the ability to see things for what they actually are, son. Don't let your mind be clouded now."

"I'm not sure what that means, but I'll take the words to heart. See ya on the flip side, Alastair Thorne."

CHAPTER 7

*H*olly stared at the colossal mahogany door of her father's palatial home. How long had it been since she'd been back here? Months and months, it seemed. And that time had only been to visit her mother's corpse-like body. Nerves ate at her belly, and the sensation felt like a thousand butterflies flitting about inside.

With a few hours left to kill before she could check into the hotel in Greece, she figured there was no point teleporting before then. She'd be stuck wandering Athens when all she really wanted to do was find Quentin and smooth things over. That gave her plenty of time to patch things up with her father—something she desperately needed to do. It was well past the point to set their relationship to rights.

Working up her courage, she banged on the door.

Nothing happened.

Again, she lifted her fist to the wood.

Nothing.

What the hell? It wasn't like her father not to be home. Not with her mother lingering in a coma in one of the upstairs bedrooms. At the very least, his manservant should be lurking about.

With a deep breath, she reached for the knob. It turned easily under her hand, and while her father had once stated she would always be welcome, Holly felt a little weird arriving unannounced.

"Hello?"

Her tentative voice echoed throughout the foyer, circling back around and making her wince at the loudness.

"Dad?"

A noise from the wide marble staircase caught her attention.

A surprised Alastair paused halfway in his descent. "Holly! Is everything all right?"

"I wanted to talk to you."

His worried expression eased, and he cast a glance upward as if to judge if he should leave Aurora.

"It's important, Dad."

The three choked-out words drew his scrutiny.

"Of course." In an out-of-character move, he ran a hand through his blond hair and mussed his perfectly coiffed do. "Tell me what you need."

"I don't need anything," she snapped. Why did everyone always assume she needed help? It was as if they couldn't believe she was capable of fending for herself.

He froze at the bottom of the stairs, and all emotion disappeared from his face. It hurt Holly's heart to see formality replace the caring his countenance had held seconds before.

"Then, once again, I'm at a loss as to how to help you." She opened her mouth to respond, but he forestalled her with a raised hand. "Hear me out, Holly."

It was the second time he'd used her given name in as many days. When had he ever called her anything but child or darling girl? The fight to hold back her tears was a hard-waged battle, but with great effort, she barely managed to win that little war.

"At every turn, you reject me. My help, my love, my money. I've tried to give you everything, to ease your plight in whatever small way I could. This is the last time. Say what you have to say, ask whatever it is you need to ask, and then go."

"Y-you don't want me to come back?" Where did that scared voice come from? It wasn't like she hadn't been on her own for years on end. Hadn't she survived Beau's betrayal and a knife to her chest? Granted, with a magical assist, but she was a strong woman, dammit! "I apologize. I guess I shouldn't have come. I don't know what I was thinking."

"You were thinking you fucked up royally with your young man." Alastair's forceful sneeze echoed around the foyer as her earlier greeting had. He clenched his hand to stave off his own particular curse—locusts. "Now you don't know how to fix it. What do you want me to say? Whatever advice I might provide, you'll do the exact opposite. Tell me, Holly, what's the point?"

Seconds ticked away as they stood staring at one another. Was it true? Did she always do the exact opposite of whatever advice he gave her? When had that started? Holly needed to swallow her pride and get on with it.

"I won't, Daddy. Please, don't send me away. I need you."

Holly couldn't see for her own tears, but the air around her moved and strong arms enveloped her in a comforting hug. For the first time since she was a small child, she let her father console her. "Please forgive me, Daddy," she sobbed.

"Shh, child. It's all right now."

"I don't hate you." When her father didn't respond, she pulled away to gaze up into his beloved face. He appeared tortured. It was as if he longed to say things but was afraid to upset the apple cart. "I don't. I know you think I do. I know I said I did, but I love you. I was being the petty bitch Quentin said I was." She didn't sneeze due to the word "bitch," and she gave him a half-smile. "Did you notice what happened there?"

"You admitted you were wrong?" he asked dryly.

"I cursed and didn't sneeze."

Surprise lit his face. "How did you discover this?"

"Summer. If we are touching, we won't sneeze. I didn't realize it could work with anyone else besides her."

"I wonder how I never discovered this?"

A wave of sadness crashed over her. She knew exactly why. Her father, the black sheep of the family and the most feared individual in the witch community, remained an island unto himself. "You'd have to touch another person to have it work. I don't imagine you let many people that close."

He drew her tightly to his chest. "Hell, you could be right." When he didn't sneeze, he laughed. "It's a sad state of affairs that this is the only way I can swear without causing a plague of locusts on mankind. Although, there are those who deserve it."

"Why did you never set the locusts on Zhu Lin's ass?"

"The magical shackles. Plus, I refused to utter a sound while being tortured."

Holly's stomach flipped. He'd never openly discussed his imprisonment during the war with the Désorcelers. Lin and his group of anti-witches had done a number on the magical population of the world. Those who may have sworn allegiance to the Thornes had been systematically wiped from the planet or turned against them with the exception of a select few. "It must have been horrific."

"It's the past. Lin is dead. Soon enough, I'll target the others involved, but I need to make sure my family is safe from repercussions and Aurora can take care of herself."

She gave him one last squeeze and backed away. "You have a plan?"

"I do."

"I want to help."

"You know I will never willingly put you in harm's way. Not after what happened with your sisters." Alastair smoothed back a lock of her wayward hair. "But I will help you and Quentin."

"I'm afraid he hates me now."

Her father's lips quirked. "You couldn't be further from the truth, child. That man would walk barefoot over burning coals for you if you asked him to."

"He really didn't cheat?"

"He really didn't. And honestly, I can't see how you could have thought he would. He can't take his eyes from you long enough to look at anyone else. The boy is a besotted fool."

Holly pressed a hand to her stomach. "It makes me sick to think I wasted all these years believing other people's lies."

"I've waited for eighteen years for your mother. Love has no expiration date."

She nodded and looked away as tears welled up again. She'd cried more in the last two days than she'd cried in her entire lifetime.

Alastair's large warm hands settled on her shoulders and gave them a light press. "You're young, and you have your whole life ahead of you. One with Quentin if either of us has a say in match-making the two of you."

A bubble of laughter unexpectedly arose with her next thought. She spun around to stare at him as the truth hit her. "You've been matchmaking all my sisters, haven't you, you old softie?"

A slow, wicked grin transformed his features. "Maybe."

"Alastair Thorne, you are one wily S.O.B."

"Don't disparage my sainted mother by calling her names," he admonished teasingly. "But you aren't wrong. Now, about your young man..."

QUENTIN CHECKED into the swanky hotel Alastair had selected, with minimal fuss. Once in his room, an odd restlessness took him. Being half a world away from Holly made his skin itch. The desire to return to her was stronger than any he'd ever experienced. And because this was so, he plunked down on the floor, crossed his legs under him, and started a deep meditation. *Started* being the key word. The insistent knocking on his door destroyed his Zen.

When it became obvious the interrupting asshat wasn't going away, he growled low in his throat and rose. He jerked open the door and came up short.

Holly.

His body's reaction was immediate. Hot, then cold, swept over him. His need to reach for her took every ounce of restraint he could manage and more. "What are you doing here? I told you to stay home."

"I'm not a dog to be ordered about," she returned sassily and slipped under the arm holding the door. "We need to set up a plan of attack."

"My plans don't include you," he snapped as he slammed the door. How the hell was he expected to seduce Selene into giving him access to the vault with Holly lurking about? He'd never be able to concentrate on the mission at hand, not when his every thought would be consumed by her.

"They do now."

As pretty as you please, she perched on the edge of the king-sized bed. And man, didn't she look magnificent sitting there? The strappy, flowing sundress showed off her lightly tanned skin to perfection. The pale pink set off her hair and added a glow to her skin. But it was her eyes, lighter than they'd been in years and focused on him with a solid purpose only she knew, that really drew him.

"I can't have you here, Holly. You should go."

"Why? Because you are supposed to make Slutty Selene fall in love with you?" She waved a hand in dismissal and crossed her legs. "We aren't going that route. I've come up with a new scheme."

The easy assumption that he would fall in with whatever she planned set him off. Quentin stalked to where she sat and squatted so they were eye level. "*You* have? Let me tell you a little fact, sweetheart. *You* no longer factor into what I do or don't do. I told your father, this one last thing, and I'm out of your life for good."

Try as she might, her brave face didn't disguise her hurt. The trembling lips knotted his guts.

"I understand." Ducking her head, she avoided looking at him.

"Do you? Because I don't think you do, Hol." He gripped her chin and forced her gaze to meet his. "I'm sick to death of loving you. If I could cut you from my heart and soul, I'd do it in a second. Showing up here is cruel and full-on bullshit."

When her lips tightened to a straight line and tears flooded her large eyes, Quentin felt like the biggest dickhead. He desperately wanted to call back his words, but doing so would throw the two of them back into the same old holding pattern where he followed her around like a faithful dog awaiting every scrap of attention.

"You don't want me anymore?"

What kind of stupid-ass question was that? Of course he wanted her. He'd go to his grave wanting her. But he was soul weary. "I can't do this anymore, Hol. I can't."

"I made a mistake. I believed Michelle. I believed she was my best friend. But she wasn't. You were. You were the one I should've believed, Quentin."

"Yes." He rose and held out a hand. "Go home, Holly. I'll bring you the scroll when I'm done."

"I'm not going. If I have to be your shadow, the way you were mine, I'll do it. You've loved me for a large chunk of our lives. The same amount of time that I loved you. You never gave up in all those years, and I'm not giving up now."

The lift of her chin, the determined gleam, and the thrown back shoulders all spoke of her resolution. Inside, he applauded her gumption. As he stared down at her, his bottomless optimism got the better of him. "You're not?"

"No." She placed a palm flat over his heart. "Never."

Her declaration of love sparked an answering vow within him—a recommitment of sorts. He'd give in. There wasn't even a question of walking away now that she'd declared her love for him. But a kernel of an idea took hold. Maybe if she had to work for *his* love for a change, she'd appreciate it all the more when he finally relented. "Not even if I seduce Selene?"

Her fingers curled into a ball against his chest, and fire flashed in her eyes. "You are *not* seducing Selene or any other woman *ever* again."

"What do you plan to do to stop it?" Quentin couldn't curb the mocking twist of his lips.

"Whatever I have to." Her hand dropped to the waistband of his jeans.

The blood rushed from his head straight to his groin. Calling on every ounce of willpower he possessed, he removed Holly's hand and turned away. If he intended to make her work for it, caving at her first provocative statement was the wrong way to go about it. He'd almost reached the door when the rustle of clothing penetrated his brain.

Closing his eyes against the image of a naked Holly, Quentin inhaled deeply. He'd forgotten how forward she could be when she wanted to be.

"Quentin."

The husky come-hither quality to her voice slayed him. He wanted nothing more than to scoop her up and bury himself so deeply inside her that he felt tomorrow. *All* their tomorrows. But sex between them would resolve nothing other than to ease his horniness.

"I have things to see to, Holly." He placed his hand on the door and faced her. The sight of her nakedness caused the skin on his entire body to tingle with want. With supreme effort, he tore his eyes away from her curvaceous figure and settled his gaze on her face. "You should go."

Disbelief, hurt, despair, and anger all warred for dominance on her countenance. "You're rejecting me?"

How did he answer? If he said yes, it would add to their problems. But wasn't he saying no in a way? "Not you, love. Your advances."

With a simple swirl of her hands, clothing once more covered her luscious body. He wanted to weep.

"It's the same thing," she snapped as she moved to pass him.

His hand shot out and gripped her upper arm to spin her back. "No, Holly, it's not. But you've rejected me for nine years. You don't get to remove your clothes and make everything all right."

"Is this payback?"

"Goodfuckingchrist!" The expletive was out before he could stop it. "How is it you can be so damned smart and yet completely oblivious?"

Angry color flooded her face. "Screw you, Quentin."

With a grip on both arms, he hauled her closer until their noses were practically touching and she stood on the tips of her toes. "*Don't!* Just don't. You have absolutely no right to be angry. *Not one!*" He gave her a light shake. "I, on the other hand, do. You constantly blew off my explanation of the encounter with Michelle. You went running into the first available arms. You refused to believe me when I said Beau was dangerous. You ignored my warning again and again. That was all in the first two years." He released her and shook his head. "The seven years that followed? Yeah, they were a picnic chasing you, trying to get you to see reason. Hoping like hell you'd forgive the imagined slights. Do you know how many pitying looks I received during those years? *Do you?*" he seethed. "I counted. From your family alone this last year, there were sixty-seven. They could all see what you and I could not. One, that I loved you, and two, that you didn't care if I lived or died as long as I was out of your hair."

Pale-faced, she shook her head. "I care. I've always cared." Her lips trembled, and she pressed them together to stop the movement.

"You sure fooled me."

"I've already apologized, Quentin," she croaked. "If I could change things, I would. But I want to move forward. With you."

Anger faded, and his heart ached at her sincerity. "As laughable as it sounds, I need time, Hol. We both do. Go back home. I'll return when I've finished here."

"You won't."

"I will."

"You told my father you were done." She came forward and placed her hands on either side of his face. "I couldn't stand it if we were."

Closing his eyes, he turned his face to plant a kiss on her palm. "Do you love me?"

"Yes."

"Then you need to learn to trust me, my prickly pear. We will never work otherwise."

CHAPTER 8

*H*olly sat on her bed later that evening and berated herself. She should never have walked out of Quentin's room. She should have stayed and made him understand that she wasn't taking no for an answer.

She touched the tanzanite stone around her neck. "Dad?"

"I'm here."

"How did you and mother work through your differences? How did you know not to give up?"

"True love doesn't allow you to give up, child. You may feel like you've barely survived a tornado, all battered and bruised with your world in shambles around you, but you dig deep for that inner strength. You rebuild a love stronger than the one that was there before."

"He sent me away."

"Give him time."

"He's furious. I had no idea how much."

"Ask yourself how you would feel. Would you be willing to forgive and forget if the situation was reversed? What if he had humiliated you time and again?"

"I didn't do that!"

"Didn't you?" After a long pause where Holly imagined she heard her father's sigh, he said, *"You may not have done it consciously, but you did it all the same. You were making him pay for a betrayal that never happened."*

Is that how they all saw it? That she'd been such a horrible person? No wonder Quentin wanted nothing more to do with her and her own father had been ready to walk away.

"I can hear your thoughts, child. I can't speak for Quentin, but I never saw you as such. I was ready to walk away for your happiness, not my own."

"Goddess, I was such an ungrateful—"

"Enough! The past is gone. Now you look forward and work toward repairing your relationship. Give him time."

"That's what he said. That he needed time."

"Then do him the courtesy of giving him what he asks for, child."

"But that would mean leaving, and that's not going to happen."

His deep chuckle resounded in her brain. *"I would expect no less from you. You're your father's child."*

"I'm taking that as a good thing, Dad."

"You should. Go order the most expensive meal room service has to offer, along with a nice vintage wine, and enjoy yourself for a change. The rest will sort itself out."

"Thank you."

"You're welcome, dear girl."

"I love you, Dad. I can't seem to say it enough."

"You could say it fifty times a day, and I would hold each and every declaration close to my heart."

"Dang! No wonder you get all the women. That was poetry, pops!"

His bark of laughter made her smile.

"Goodnight, dear."

"Goodnight, Dad."

"Oh, and Holly?"

"Yeah?"

"I love you, too."

She felt the second their mental connection was broken, but still, she would carry the warmth of their conversation through the remainder of the day. It reminded her of the times when she'd been a small child. Her father had always been there with open arms, ready to pick her up when she fell down. Why hadn't she remembered that before now? Why had she let hurt and anger become the cornerstone of their relationship?

Now, their relationship was on its way to being repaired. For that, she was grateful.

One down, one more to go.

Her phone lit up with a text from Quentin. *"Want to join me for dinner tonight?"*

She smiled and tapped out an affirmative reply.

The screen brightened again. *"Wear a pretty dress and be ready in fifteen minutes."*

Holly was ready in seven. The remaining eight minutes were spent in an agony of nerves. Somehow, she had to force Quentin to see she was serious about making a go of things. Make him see she'd always loved him even if her actions stated otherwise. The thought of him leaving—that he might be through with the whole tangled mess—made her heart ache in a way she hadn't allowed in years. Until now, she'd closed her emotions off. Allowing even a smidgen of her feelings for him inside had been too painful.

A knock sounded on the connecting door. Quentin stood dressed in black slacks and a white button-down shirt. He'd left his long, dark hair loose. Although Quentin wore modern clothing, Holly was reminded of the pirates of old with their flowing shirts and devil-may-care attitudes.

His gaze was bold as he took in her appearance. The appreciative look in his eyes warmed her and chased away the bulk of her misgivings. When their gazes connected, her breath caught in her chest.

"As always, you're stunning." His husky baritone reached right in and set fire to Holly's woman cave.

"As always, your own beauty is god-like."

His grin flashed, and he stepped over the threshold to her room. He didn't stop until his chest was pressed to hers. "Is that right?"

"You know it is. You possess a mirror."

He raised a brow but remained quiet and watchful.

"I guess that was snarky." She sighed and placed the flat of her palm over his heart. "I didn't mean it to be. I guess it's harder to erase habits than I thought."

Quentin covered her hand with his, then raised it to place a kiss on her fingertips. "I know. But I need to get used to this new Holly."

"I've been horrible to you for too long, Quentin. I'm more sorry than I can say."

"I know that, too, Hol. You don't need to say it again."

"But I do. I've been swimming in an ocean of lies for such a long time; I didn't always know what was true or false. Never once did I recognize that you were my life preserver; right there in front of me the whole time, waiting for me to grab hold." She caught back the emotion threatening to erupt. "You always kept me safe in spite of myself and my ridiculous temper."

"I love you, Holly Thorne. I will love you until my dying day. But we need to establish a bridge of trust between us."

"You want to be with me?" She hated the hesitation and insecurity in her own voice.

"More than I want to breathe, my prickly pear." Quentin lowered his head until his lips were a hairsbreadth away from hers. "You have always been the beacon of light in my dark sky."

His kiss, when it came, chased all thought from her head and curled her toes—just as it always had. Holly sagged into Quentin and inched her hands up around his neck. When his arms encircled her, she sighed her contentment. *This* was right. *This* was exactly where she needed to be and who she needed to be with.

He drew back with one last lingering kiss. "Let's talk more over dinner."

"Okay. But I think you should know, I'm not leaving you to do this alone. I'm going to help retrieve the scroll."

"Why am I not surprised?"

Without warning, her humor took hold and a smirk forced its way onto her lips. "I bet I can still surprise you."

He mock shuddered. "The prospect is terrifying."

They shared a long, meaningful look. For the first time in forever, Holly felt a sense of rightness.

"I trust you, Quentin."

A pained expression came and went over his face.

"What?"

"I'm not sure I trust you, Hol."

She winced even as he said it. Bile rose in the back of her throat, and all her old insecurities came back to haunt her. Was she that difficult?

"I can already see you've taken my words the wrong way." He sighed and tilted up her chin. "I should say, I don't trust in your trust."

"What the hell does that mean?" She promptly sneezed and released a relieved sigh when he clenched his fist. He always anticipated her affliction and counteracted her curse.

"I don't trust that when the chips are down, you won't find a reason to believe the worst of me again. That you won't take someone else's word against mine."

"Well, believe it," she snapped.

His lips twitched as his eyes lit with merriment.

"And don't you dare laugh at me!"

"I wouldn't dream of it. The Thorne temper is a scary sight to behold. I certainly wouldn't want to be on the receiving end."

"Oh, shut it." She grabbed her purse from the table by the couch. "Let's go. I'm starving."

"Your wish is my command."

"Pfft. As if!"

He halted their progress toward the door. "Care to explain that?"

"My wish was to do the dirty earlier. That didn't get me anywhere."

Quentin burst out laughing.

Holly wanted the floor to open and swallow her whole. Where

was her sister Spring's ability to part the earth when she needed it? And why the hell had she confessed to being irritated that he hadn't accepted her advances?

All the way to the lobby, Holly fumed and wondered why she'd suddenly become filterless. Mere days ago, she wouldn't have dreamed of confessing to wanting him. On the other hand, before Quentin lay recovering on her couch, she didn't have all the facts. The knowledge that he'd saved her made the difference. Now she knew exactly to what extreme he would go for her.

A shiver traveled the length of her spine.

"You okay?" Ever attentive, Quentin had picked up on her body's reaction to her own thoughts.

"I was thinking about our conversation the other day in my living room."

He nodded as if he understood exactly to which conversation she referred. "Now you fear me?"

She jerked to a halt. "What? *No!*"

His questioning gaze bore into her, seeking the truth. Finally, relief settled on his features, and he nodded.

"Quentin, you can't possibly believe I would ever fear you. You've been there for me every step of the way."

"I worried that if you found out the truth, you would view me differently."

"I do, but not in the way you think. You're my hero. You saved my life that night."

He grimaced, and the flash of discomfort told Holly more than his words ever could.

"Quentin, look at me." She waited for him to meet her steady gaze. "You truly *are* a hero. I don't know what more you think you could have done, but I wasn't likely to heed any warnings. And you *did* try to warn me."

"I should've tried harder to get you to listen."

"To what end? You might have averted their plan that night, but they might have tried again, and possibly succeeded because you weren't around to stop them."

This time, he was the one who shivered. "I don't want to contemplate what might have happened. Can we let it go now?"

"In a minute." She wrapped her arms around his middle and rested her forehead over his heart. "I need to thank you properly. I need you to understand how much I appreciate what you did for me. But mostly, I need you to understand how much I love you. How much I've always loved you."

When Quentin's arms tightened around her in a reflexive response to her words, Holly sighed. She had to believe they could work through the trust issue and come out stronger on the other side. Letting him walk away now wasn't an option.

Her stomach growled and ruined the moment.

She felt Quentin's deep chuckle where her forehead was pressed against him.

"Let's get you fed before you turn back into a prickly pear."

"I've never not been prickly according to you," she retorted good-naturedly with a light slap on his broad chest.

"I wouldn't have you any other way."

"You say that now. But in another twenty years, you'll wish for a woman with a sunnier disposition."

"Never."

She hid her pleased smile. "Feed me."

"With pleasure."

CHAPTER 9

*Q*uentin recognized Selene the second she stepped through the door. Based on the information Alastair had provided, Selene arrived at this particular restaurant every Wednesday evening at eight o'clock.

Holly had excused herself to use the restroom two minutes ago, which left Quentin with roughly three to make Selene's acquaintance and set into action the plan to retrieve the scroll.

Since Holly's arrival in Greece, he'd been wondering how the hell he was going to pull off a seduction. Not only did he not want to jeopardize the tentative bond re-forming between him and Holly, he couldn't work up the desire for another woman. It was as if Holly owned him, mind, body, and soul.

He studied Selene from his seat, facing the entrance. She was a vision in white. Tall, at roughly five-foot-ten, Selene had the lean elegance of a model and moved with a fluid grace, no gesture wasted. Watching her walk was almost like watching a ballerina in motion. Her thick black hair was pulled into a chignon with a few strategic curls allowed to escape. Diamond drops dangled from delicate ears and accentuated her perfect jawline and slender neck.

But it was her eyes that drew the most notice. Their shape was emphasized by the modern smoky-eye makeup technique. From across the room, it was impossible to determine the color of her eyes although Quentin already knew they would be a dark brown based on the dossier. When those eyes fastened on him, his stomach sank. There was no mistaking the interested gleam. It was followed closely by determination.

Selene changed her trajectory, abandoning the *maître d'* and veering straight for Quentin's table. She stopped shy of touching him.

"Well, hello, lover."

"Ma'am."

Her mouth tightened on the word ma'am.

He almost grinned. He wasn't sure what it said about him that he liked needling people.

Selene composed herself and affected a sultry expression. "I haven't seen you around here before."

"It's my first visit."

"It seems sad to dine alone. I invite you to join me."

The back of his neck tingled—a clear indication Holly was near. "I'm not alone. I'm with my girlfriend."

Holly's response was to gently weave her hand into the hair at the back of his head and massage his scalp.

His challenging gaze never left Selene's, who refused to acknowledge Holly's return.

"You are more than welcome to join us if you'd like."

Quentin whipped his head around so fast he almost got whiplash. He could do nothing but gape at Holly's friendly offer. A smile teased her lips, and a devilish gleam danced in her eyes. *What the hell was she up to?*

"Thank you, but no," Selene returned coolly. "Enjoy your meal."

Once Selene had departed, Holly dropped her hand. When she moved to walk away, Quentin grabbed her wrist and drew her back. Words weren't needed as they stared at one another.

With a suddenness that surprised him, she bent and placed her lips against his. She pulled back with a wide grin. "I'm your girl-friend, huh?"

"That's the way I've always seen it."

"Good to know. Have you ordered yet?"

"Hol, what was that?"

"Staking my claim?"

"I meant the invitation to Selene. What are you about?"

"Quentin, why did you bring me here tonight?"

Any answer he gave at this point would go over like a lead balloon. Holly wouldn't believe him if he said he wanted to take her someplace nice—which was partially true.

"You brought me here because you knew she'd be here, didn't you?"

"Yes."

Her eyes flashed with her outrage before she focused her attention over his shoulder. "You should go have dinner with her. I'll see you back at the hotel."

"Don't!" When she turned to go, he rose and reached for her. A deep-rooted need on his part refused to let her walk away. "Please stay and have dinner with me."

The eyes she turned up to him were no longer angry. Instead, they held a profound sadness. "Coming to Greece was a bad idea. I should have stayed home."

"Maybe. But you're here now, love."

"I'm only going to hinder your plans, Quentin. In doing that, I hinder my mother's recovery." She took a shaky breath. "Which choice do I make? Stand back while you screw another woman, or let my mother languish in her stasis?"

"This goes back to the trust issue, Holly. Either you believe in me or you don't."

"You have no intention of sleeping with her?"

He remained silent, willing her to have faith in him.

Once again, her eyes darted behind him. "I can't blame you if you do. She's gorgeous. Much prettier than I am." She swallowed hard. "I've not been there for you. I didn't have enough faith in us as a couple to believe you over Michelle."

There was a heartbreaking quality to her voice, and it pained Quentin. He wanted to assure her that he'd still be there for her forever. Yet, he wasn't sure he could be. At least not until they worked through their problems, and that would take more than a single shared meal.

"Can we take this one day at a time?" He asked softly. "Have dinner with me, love. Let's enjoy our first night in Greece without any agendas."

She turned tear-bright eyes in his direction. "Okay."

He guided her to her chair and held it out for her. Once she was seated, he handed her the menu and lingered beside her long enough to say, "For the record, you are much prettier than she is. To me, you are the most beautiful woman on the planet. Appetizer?"

HOLLY FOUND herself sneaking peeks at Selene throughout dinner. The woman was a sexy goddess in human form. Never had Holly felt more inferior in her entire life. Yet, she detected no guile in Quentin's words when he said she was much prettier. To his mind, he truly believed it.

More than once, she caught his contemplative gaze studying her. Nervousness ate away at any confidence she may have gained over the years of being an independent woman. Why did she continually doubt her own worth?

"Dessert?"

She jumped when Quentin spoke. Silence seemed to have reigned for the better part of their dinner. It wasn't how she'd imagined the evening going when he first texted her earlier.

"Can we get it to go? I'd like to see Athens by moonlight."

His warm smile sent her pulse racing.

After he paid the tab, they strolled hand-in-hand through town. Although Athens was a blend of old world and new, the place resonated within her. The roughly paved streets, the red tiled roofs, even the graffiti on the side of a few of the buildings were so different from everything she was used to. Here was a place with over half-a-million residents, and yet she liked it. Each building had a story. Was the rest of Europe similar?

"Have you ever been anywhere other than home?"

"Yes." He surprised her with his answer.

Jerking to a halt, she gaped up at him. "Really? When?" A small kernel of hurt took hold. During the year they were together, they discussed their dreams of exploring the world together. She hadn't given much consideration to him going without her.

"While you were married." A muscle ticked in his jaw. "I had nothing but time on my hands."

"Quentin, if I could go back and redo—"

"You can't. There is no use living in the past, Hol."

"But I feel as if you haven't truly forgiven me." The confession cost her, and she suspected the crack in her whispered voice gave her away.

"And if I haven't?"

She raised her eyes to meet his probing gaze. "It might break my heart."

"Might, Hol?"

"Will."

"I forgave you years ago. What I found harder to dismiss was your stubborn refusal to listen. Things can't always be your way, love."

"I know that!"

"Do you?" He sighed and tugged her into his arms. "Let's not fight. Not tonight. Tonight, let's pretend we are two strangers meeting for the first time." He kissed the crown of her head. "We'll discuss topics as if we're just getting to know one another. Maybe talk about future dreams. What do you say?"

"I'd like that."

She lifted her head, but not before she pressed her nose close to his chest and inhaled. Oh, how she loved the faint mixture of sandalwood and fresh, clean soap that was unique to him. His scent had the ability to calm and excite her at the same time.

"How is it that you always smell divine?"

His laughter rumbled through his chest; she felt it where she pressed against him. "That information is for our second date."

She bit her lip to curb her smile. Quentin's charm was legendary, and she refused to feed his ego. It was much better to keep him on his toes if she could.

"Back to your original question; I spent time in Ireland. At first, I kicked around Dublin, haunting pub after pub, drowning my sorrows. But self-pity can only be tolerated so long. When I resolved to not be a pathetic asshat for the remainder of my life, I explored the rest of the country. After about six months, I set off to backpack across Europe."

"I think I dislike you a little right now."

He grinned down at her. "I made a long list of all the places I wanted to show you. Does that get me out of the doghouse?"

She held up her index finger and thumb with about an inch of space between the two.

"I'll have to work harder," he quipped.

"Where is the first place you'd take me?"

"The Cliffs of Moher are incredible. I think I'd take you there first."

"Pfft. I wouldn't trust that you wouldn't throw me off."

"There's that word again—trust."

Holly winced. "I didn't mean it like that. I was trying to tease."

"I know. Seems I'm the prickly one lately, huh?"

"You can be my prickly pear this time around."

He chuckled and led her down the ancient streets.

They made it about five feet when he halted and spun around. His eyes darted here and there, taking in their surroundings. "We're being watched."

Maybe it was his warning, but Holly experienced an odd ripple, indicating the presence of another witch or warlock. She lowered her voice for only his ears. "Should we teleport?"

"Let's get to the shadows on the left. It might provide enough cover to hide what we can do."

Before they took a step, Holly's half-brother stepped from a nearby alley and waved them over.

"*Nash?* What's going on?"

"There's a buzz about the Witches' Council that something big is going down here in Athens. Alastair wants you to abandon this little project." He looked grim which didn't bode well for whatever drama was unfolding.

She shook her head. "No. We need that scroll."

"Christ, Holly, you are stubborn to a fault."

Nash's harsh comment had Quentin glowering and stepping closer.

"Call off your watchdog," Nash ordered with heavy disgust.

"I've got your watchdog," Quentin growled.

Nash, contrary as only a Thorne could be, smirked and winked at Quentin. "Down, boy."

Because the little devil inside her appreciated Nash's needling, Holly bit back her own smirk.

"Seriously, we aren't leaving. Let's get back to the hotel and discuss what's happening. I'm not comfortable being exposed on the street if there truly is an event going down."

She grabbed Quentin's and Nash's hands. Visualizing her large open suite, she teleported them to her hotel room.

"A little warning would be nice next time." Nash dusted off an imaginary speck of dirt from his shoulder.

Holly giggled.

Although he'd never admit it, her brother was a replica of her father. Acerbic wit, mannerisms, and all.

"Spill your guts, brother. What do you know?"

"Only what I said. The Witches' Council wants everyone back on their respective continents. That goes doubly so for Thornes because they believe we are behind a good eighty percent of the problems that cross their desk. Alastair thinks you should pay heed and come home."

Quentin shook his head. "Not going to happen. We've come to get the scroll that could save Aurora. You can help or leave, but we aren't going home without it."

Pleased to know he had her back, Holly threaded her fingers within his. "Thank you."

His answer was a tightening of his hand over hers.

"Sister, you need to listen to me. The Council wouldn't issue an order if there wasn't a reason."

"I don't care, Nash. This is our last chance to save my mother. If you'd seen her…" Holly cleared her throat. The memory from a few months back, of seeing her mother with her gray pallor, wasting away to nothing, was difficult at best. "I have to try."

For the span of roughly ten beats, Nash studied her. His countenance revealed nothing of his thoughts. It unnerved her to a large degree. His resemblance to Alastair was uncanny. Thoughts of her father sent her hand to clutch the tanzanite stone at the base of her throat.

"I'll help you. But if you tell our sperm donor of my involvement, there will be revenge the likes you've never experienced before. Got it?"

"Is now a bad time to tell him that I heard everything?" Her father's dry comment came through their telepathic connection loud and clear, and Holly nearly snorted aloud.

"Got it." She told Nash. "I appreciate this more than you know."

"Yeah, well, I'm taking your room because this place is sold out. You can bunk with lover boy."

Quentin, who had been quiet for most of Nash's visit, spoke. "If you didn't plan to stay, how do you know they were sold out?"

"Smart boy!" Her father approved. *"He's a thinker, that one."*

Instead of being defensive, Nash laughed.

"You planned to help us all along, didn't you?" Holly asked.

"Since when has a Thorne listened to reason? It's not like I could leave you here alone." Nash flashed her a mischievous grin. "And if it puts Alastair's nose out of joint that I didn't usher you both right back home—bonus!"

"I'm not alone. I have Quentin."

Her brother's amused jade gaze moved between them. "Yes, he's like a barnacle you can't remove, isn't he?"

Holly shook her head. "I'm going to dance a jig the day you fall in love, Nash. And I hope she leads you on a merry chase."

A shuttered look took the place of his lightheartedness. It was a clear indication he already had experience in the love department and perhaps hadn't fared well.

"Who is she?"

"None of your damned business."

"Mmhmm. Don't think I won't ferret it out."

"Ask him about his assistant." Alastair inserted, nearly causing her to jump. Holly had forgotten he was listening in.

"Let it go, sister."

"With all the long hours you put in at Thorne Industries, I'd say it's a coworker," she teased. "Maybe an assistant?"

His dark look confirmed her query. "How about we get back to what's important?"

"Holly has to dance her jig first," Quentin said dryly. He leaned in to whisper in her ear. "Personally, I find the idea of you dancing very important—and intriguing."

A fiery blush spread up her neck and face. "I'm with Nash; we need to discuss the Council issue." Holly was almost certain she heard a deep chuckle through her psychic connection with Alastair. Embarrassment made her drop the necklace like a hot rock. Quentin echoed her father's chuckle. Apparently, he had a good idea what the stone could do.

She elbowed him in the ribs. "Shut it and have a seat, you tool. My neck hurts looking up at you."

"This should make us more level." In a move that surprised a squeak from her, he swept her into his arms and settled onto the couch with her firmly ensconced on his lap.

"He's a smooth one." Nash's laughter mingled with theirs.

Because in Quentin's arms was exactly where she wanted to be,

Holly didn't squirm or struggle. Instead, she leaned back into his chest and enjoyed the closeness.

"Explain what's going on with the Council, Nash. We have the right to know what we're getting into by staying," Quentin said.

Her brother sat in one of the two armchairs across from them. "Information about the Cheirotonia Scroll and Alastair's need of it has come to light. It's no secret the Council isn't his biggest fan."

"They sent you to stop us?"

"Initially they came to me," he said by way of confirming Holly's suspicion. "I told them no. But that only means they'll alert a contact on this side of the world."

"Selene."

Holly twisted to face Quentin. "Do you suppose that's why she approached you in the restaurant? That she already knows who you are?"

"It's a possibility."

"Then how are you going to get in good with her?"

He squinted in Nash's direction. "Any hope that Selene Barringer might *not* be the person they turn to?"

Nash shook his head. "But she doesn't know me. We could formulate a new plan."

"I don't think that would work, brother. As much as you detest the fact, you are almost the spitting image of our father. Even your mannerisms resemble his."

"Yeah, I've been told." The grimace on his face told everyone he resented any comments to that effect. "However, I can alter my appearance."

"I need to be the one to get the scroll."

"Quentin, I appreciate what you are trying to do for my mother, but—"

"No, love. I *need* to be the one. If I don't touch that scroll, I can't save you from Beau and Michelle."

CHAPTER 10

"*W*hat the hell are you talking about? *Achoo!*"

Quentin raised his fist to magically stem off an avian attack on the building. Holly's fierce question triggered an equally fierce result. When he was certain an influx of birds wasn't imminent, he faced brother and sister. Their twin looks of confusion were about to turn to disbelief when he revealed what he knew about the past and the scroll.

"First and foremost, I'm not crazy. We should establish that right from the get-go." He sighed when Holly scrunched up her face in concern. "Second, I'm not sure how it worked for my future self, but the night Holly was assaulted by Beau and Michelle, it was future me who came and warned me it was going to happen."

"What? How can there be two of you, and what do you mean by future you?"

In order to convey his seriousness, he looked Holly dead in the eye. "I came back from the future to make sure you didn't wind up a corpse that night."

She scrambled off his lap, and her look of horror was a clear indication she thought he'd snapped.

"Hol, I'm not nuts." Quentin rose and moved toward her. When she backed away, hands in the air, he sighed his frustration. A quick glance in Nash's direction showed that at least her brother considered the idea of time travel possible. "Please keep an open mind while I explain." At Nash's nod, he continued, "Future me came to the restaurant earlier that night. He cornered me before I walked through the door and told me everything. Or at least everything having to do with the attack."

Quentin frowned as he tried to recall what was said that night.

"I swear, I thought I was having a psychotic break. But he told me things that hadn't happened yet. Told me minute-by-minute details of how the next two hours would go. He made me promise if it all went down like he said it would, if she left with Beau after he grabbed her arm and tried to haul her away, I was to head to a specific address." He faced Holly. "That address was for the cabin Beau took you to. All of it was a result of the scroll, Hol. It's why I need it. I'm now future me, and I have to go back to warn past me."

She shook her head and looked at her brother.

"I get that this is insane, love. But that parchment has strong magic. He told me that, too."

"Did future you tell you how the heck you were supposed to get it?" Nash asked.

"You're buying into this craziness, Nash?"

Quentin moved in front of Holly and stared down into her alarmed gaze. "I thought you said you trusted me."

"I want to…" Her eyes shot to Nash again.

"I see." Disappointment rode Quentin hard. Because he couldn't bear to see the apprehension in Holly's eyes, he moved to the window. He stared out over Athens, not seeing any of the city's beauty.

For a few hours today, he'd thought maybe he and Holly stood a chance. Now, he knew differently. Now, he knew why future Quentin refused to reveal any details other than, together, they saved her life. In the end, no matter how much his romantic soul wanted to be the one who got the girl, in all likelihood, it wouldn't come to pass. Their differences were too great.

"Quentin, please understand," Holly said from beside him. "This all sounds so... so..."

He didn't spare her a glance, only continued to stare unseeingly out toward the lit Parthenon in the distance. "Insane? Yeah, I know, Hol."

When Holly's hand settled on his lower back, he flinched. He wanted to yell. Wanted to tell her to keep her damned hands to herself. At the same time, he wanted to turn to her and pull her close, never letting her go. For that reason, he stepped away and returned to the sofa.

Perching on the edge, he balanced his elbows on his knees and clasped his hands in front of him to address Nash. "I'm sure you think I'm nuts, too. But what else can you tell me about the scroll? Was there any indication as to how the Council found out about our mission?"

Nash's penetrating stare made Quentin squirm inside. With a concerted effort, he maintained eye contact, shoving all the confidence he didn't feel into a single look as he waited for Nash to respond.

"As a matter of fact, there was a whisper of a rumor that someone used the scroll to bend time. No one knows where or how the rumor started."

"There are witches and warlocks who can bend time at will. How is this different?" Holly settled in the armchair beside Nash.

"Witches and warlocks have been known to *stop* time for mere seconds, sister. Bending time, messing with the whole time-continuum, and returning to the past? Yeah, that's not normal and a whole other matter entirely. One that concerns the Powers That Be."

"He's not crazy?"

Swift rage flooded Quentin. His frayed temper finally snapped. "I'm right here, Holly!"

Her hand flew up toward her mouth.

"She didn't mean—"

"Yes, she damned well did." He'd had enough and cut Nash off.

"Let Holly keep her suite, and you take my room, Nash. I have a few things to see to. I'll meet up with you both over breakfast."

"Quentin!" Holly's cry fell on deaf ears.

Quentin didn't wait for apologies or explanations. He didn't dare. Not when the walls were closing in on him and his skin felt too small for his body. There was no telling what he would say in his anger.

With a clear image of the Temple of Athena, he closed his eyes, letting the magic heat his cells to almost burning. After arriving at his destination, he surveyed the area and berated himself for not sending out a magical feeler first. It was by the Goddess's good grace that no one was present when he teleported to this location.

Taking a deep, cleansing breath, he approached the columns where the ancient power of the place called to him. The spirits of the old Greek gods and goddesses still lingered in the very air he breathed. He bowed his head as a sign of respect.

When the oppressive air lifted, Quentin moved forward and touched the stone column closest to him. This historic ruin was the perfect representation of how old and tired he felt. Should he feel this world weary at only twenty-nine years of age? He could only imagine how Alastair must feel. The man was three-quarters of a century old. He'd seen the seedier side of life, been subjected to countless tortures at the hands of two madmen, and suffered without the love of his life for the better part of twenty years. Yet, through it all, Alastair had remained optimistic in his droll, arrogant way. As matchmaker to five couples, he had to have an element of the romantic soul himself, didn't he?

Quentin sat. With his back to the column, he surveyed the horizon. There lay Athens; its bustling city on the verge of sleep, lights winking out even as he watched.

Tomorrow, he would be forced to meet with the Thorne siblings and devise a plan to retrieve the object he needed to save Holly and that Alastair needed to save Aurora Fennell-Thorne.

The similarities weren't lost on him. Alastair loved a woman who wasn't even his wife, but the wife of another, yet he would do whatever it took to save her life. Just as Quentin had done... er, would do.

Yeah, the whole thing was a muddle. He didn't blame Holly for thinking he was off his rocker.

Added to the mess now was the Witches' Council.

"Why the hell wasn't my future self more clear on how I'm expected to go about all this shit?" he muttered as he thunked his head back against the stone.

"Because your future self knew you had a tough decision to make."

Quentin was up and shooting an icy blast of air in the direction of the newcomer before she'd finished her sentence. The force of his power scarcely ruffled her dark, upswept hair.

"Nicely done, child, but ineffective on a goddess of my stature." She smiled, and it warmed a place he didn't know was cold. Perhaps it was her blue eyes so similar to Holly's in color, or maybe it was her open, friendly demeanor, but Quentin found himself mesmerized by the goddess before him.

"Forgive me, Exalted One." He dropped to one knee in a show of deference.

"You may rise." She glided forward, and the folds of her dress sparkled, reflecting the moonlight in its shimmering silver strands. "My, you are a tall one, Quentin Buchanan. Do you know who I am?"

"Since I'm standing in Athens, am I to assume you are Athena?"

Her laughter was musical in nature. "I'm impressed. Most would assume I am Nike. Throughout history, we've been confused."

He shot her a half grin. "I can't say I'm up on my Greek history. A failing for sure."

Again, she laughed. "I like you, child. You have a boldness not seen in a lot of mortals these days."

"I am honored."

"I can see you truly mean that." Athena's head shifted slightly to the left as she studied him. "You have a warrior's heart."

"Thank you. That means a lot coming from you."

"You also have the soul of a poet and true romantic."

"I would call it a sucker for love, but I won't argue."

A broad smile graced her lips. "I see you have a humorous retort for every compliment. Why is that, do you suppose?"

He grinned in response to her smile. He was helpless against her beauty and charm. "I can't say for certain."

"I'm sure you could, but let us get back to your original question."

His mind went blank. What the hell had he asked?

"Your future self," she reminded him gently.

"Ah, yes. I was lamenting the fact he hadn't told me more about this part of my life and how I was to get what I need."

"Like I said, you have a decision to make."

Together they stood overlooking the city named for her, letting the weight of her words sink in.

"I don't know how to do that," he finally admitted. "I don't know how to choose between going back to save her and starting this cycle all over again, or making sure I never meet her in order for her to live her life without pain." He scrubbed his face with his hands. "It seems as if it should be a simple choice, doesn't it? I should sacrifice our time together." He rubbed a hand over his heart where he felt a widening crack at the idea of walking away from Holly. "But that year and a half we were together has carried me through until now. Hope springs eternal."

"A difficult decision to be sure."

"May I ask you a question?"

"Of course."

"How many times have we been here, you and I? How many times have I stood on this very spot, asking you in which direction I should go?"

She shifted and turned her solemn, wise eyes on him. "Time is a continuous loop. Humans rarely vary from their choices because they let emotion rule them."

"You aren't going to tell me, are you?"

"We've stood in this spot and replayed this exact conversation over three-hundred times on this plane or another."

Stunned stupid, he could only stare.

"You always follow your heart, Quentin. You are true and strong, and it is why I come back to visit with you every time. You inspire me."

"Does any of it work out in my favor in the end?"

"Is that a requirement for doing the right thing?"

He dropped his gaze and studied the worn stone at their feet. Was it? "No. No, it isn't. I'll save Holly no matter what it takes."

"Like I said, the heart of a warrior."

He decided to ask the question that had been burning at the back of his brain since he learned of the scroll's existence. "Is there any guarantee she won't meet and marry Beau if I remove myself from the equation?"

"No."

Quentin dropped his chin to his chest and inhaled deeply. He'd already guessed at the answer but to hear it spoken aloud was rough.

"But the Fates can be guided."

He whipped his head around at the first sign of hope. "Would you do that for me?"

"I will wait to see what you decide." Athena placed a petal-soft hand along his jaw. "Perhaps it is time for you to break the cycle, child."

Unexpected tears burned behind his lids, and he closed his eyes against the sting. He'd only ever cried once before; the day Holly lay bleeding from her knife wound. But as emotion choked him now, he wished there were a better way. How could one man be so cursed as to lose everything and everyone he ever loved? First his parents as a small boy, then Holly as a young man, and now, once again, he was faced with having to walk away from her. Could he stand to lose her for good?

He voiced none of his pain, but he suspected Athena understood all the same. The gruffness was a dead giveaway of his inner turmoil when he said, "Thank you for your guidance, Exalted One."

"Come, I will show you my favorite spot, and we shall have wine and break bread together. You will fall in love with my city."

When Athena held out her arm, he didn't hesitate to place her hand on his forearm and guide her, as would a gentleman of old.

"Should I be wary of eating or drinking anything from your world? Like the faeries, will I be enslaved?"

Her musical laughter echoed off the stones of the temple. "Would you care to be?"

"For you? Hell, yeah!"

"Quentin Buchanan, I believe you are what is referred to in your time as an incorrigible flirt."

He chuckled and allowed himself to be carefree for the remainder of the night. Tomorrow's tough choices would come all too soon.

CHAPTER 11

"*Where the hell have you been? Achoo!*"

Holly sounded like a shrill fishwife even to her own ears. So much for trying to remain calm and collected. She had planned to, but as the minutes turned to hours and the dawn lit the room through the windows, her practiced patience turned sour and eventually disintegrated. The second he appeared, she lost her shit.

Neither she nor Quentin anticipated her violent curse, and as a result, no less than thirty ravens settled on the balcony railing. En masse, their hoarse caws were deafening.

"Goddess!" Nash shouted through the open connecting doors from the other room. "Holly, curb your tongue, woman, or we will all be pecked to death."

"Shut it!" she shouted in return, before turning her furious gaze on Quentin. "What the he—"

"Careful, Hol. You're working up to an epic temper tantrum."

She stormed to where he stood and punched his chest. She'd have aimed for his damned throat had she been tall enough. For that matter, why hadn't she ever practiced levitation?

"Were you with *her*?"

"Her?" His dumbfounded expression told her he had no idea where she was coming from.

"Her. *Selene,*" she ground out.

His confused expression cleared, and he carefully blanked his features. "No. Not *her.*"

But he had been with a female. He wouldn't have replied the way he had if he'd spent the night alone. That much Holly knew.

Her heart seized in her chest, and she found it difficult to breathe. She had no rights where he was concerned. She had destroyed any claim she had on him years ago, but it still hurt that he could casually disregard her feelings.

Holly spun away to hide her upset. She didn't dare give in to her pain. If she did, she might break apart and ruin the whole mission. Careful to keep her voice neutral, she asked, "Do you need to catch a few hours of sleep before we order breakfast, or do you want to get the planning for the scroll retrieval out of the way first?"

"I'll take a nap after breakfast. We can't do anything before nightfall anyway." She heard his sigh behind her. "I wasn't with anyone else last night, Holly. Not the way you think anyway."

"You don't know what I think, Quentin. You always assume you do, but you don't."

"I'd ask if you care to enlighten me, but I'm not up for the argument right now. I have too much weighing on me today. Conjure or order what you and Nash want for breakfast. I'll eat whatever is left over after my shower."

She turned as he stalked toward the *en suite* bathroom. A large part of her wanted to rush after him. To beg his forgiveness for her adverse reaction to his time-travel claims last night. But an even bigger part understood he needed time to get over his pique with her.

"Quentin!"

He halted but didn't face her.

"I don't truly believe you are crazy. It's only that the idea of time travel seems far out to me. Very Sci-Fi and unreal, ya know?"

He nodded once and started to walk away.

"I'm sorry."

This time when he stopped, he spun back around and glared. The air crackled with energy, and the curtains to her right swayed from his elemental magic. "You're always sorry, Hol. How about you stop doing stupid shit to be sorry for?"

His rage was a slap in the face, and Holly reared back as if physical contact had taken place. Her mouth opened and closed on the words to defend herself, but he wasn't wrong. She was ninety-nine-point-nine percent to blame for their relationship problems.

"Do you know how many times we've had this discussion?" He stormed to where she stood. *"Do you?"*

"We've never had this discussion, Quentin." She had no idea what he was getting at, but for the second time in the last ten hours, she suspected he'd lost his mind. "You've never been this angry with me before."

"Yes, I have. I may not have said the words, but I've been plenty angry with you, sweetheart," he told her, sparing nothing. "But I'm talking about *this* moment in time. Standing in *this* hotel room with your brother next door, trying not to charge in here and rip my throat out for talking to you this way."

The temptation to see if Nash was behind her was strong, but she curbed the impulse. Slowly, she shook her head. "No. I don't know."

"Over three hundred according to the Goddess Athena. Let that sink in, Hol. That means for three-hundred-plus cycles, you and I have come to this place in time. For three-hundred-plus cycles, you believed I wronged you, you married another man, and I've had to get that damned scroll to start the cycle all over again to save your ungrateful ass."

His scathing words lacerated her heart. They stung because it sounded like he wished he hadn't had to be here at all, as if saving her from Beau and Michelle's evilness was a chore.

Suddenly it was all too much to deal with. She was tired of the push and pull of emotions. Tired of being considered such an unpleasant person that people found being around her a difficult duty.

"Then don't," she found herself saying. "Don't save me, Quentin.

It's not your job. Let them finish what they started."

"Ah, hell!" His large hand wrapped around her neck and hauled her close. Putting his forehead to hers, he closed his eyes. His anger seemingly gone. "I can't do that, Hol. I could never do that. *Never.*" His ragged sigh made her stomach flip-flop. "Goddess, I love you, Holly. More than you will ever know. If we have to do this ridiculous dance for eternity, then that's what we'll do. Because I could never knowingly let anyone hurt you."

She sobbed his name, and he drew her closer still.

"Shhh. It's okay, love. Don't cry."

She cried anyway. A big, ugly, snotty cry that would scare most men away.

Quentin bent and lifted her, tucking her against his chest. In the back of her mind, she heard the door shut between the suites as Quentin settled on the bed and cradled her in his arms.

"You're killing me, Hol. Don't cry. I can't stand to see you cry." He kissed each eyelid and rubbed her back even as he rocked her like a small child. "Don't cry."

"I l-love y-you, Q-Quentin," she managed through hiccupping sobs. "I-I'm so s-sorry."

His arms tightened. "It's all right, love. I promise, it's all right."

"Y-you're right. I'm s-stupid!"

"You're not stupid. Not the least little bit. I was being an ass." He dropped a lingering kiss on her forehead and conjured tissues to gently mop up her face. "Besides, I said you do stupid shit. Not that you're stupid. There's a huge difference between the two," he tried to tease.

"Over the two years of our marriage, Beau continually undermined me. Basically, he gaslighted me and had me believing I was less than I should be. Less than who I once was when you and I were together." She inhaled a ragged breath. "You always made me feel special and smart."

"You *are* smart, love. That internal dialogue is Beau in your head. Don't go there."

"I don't feel smart. I didn't see that the people closest to me had systematically set out to hurt me. Beau and Michelle made me question my intelligence and destroyed my relationships with my family. With *you*." It was an effort, but she shoved aside her embarrassment and lifted her head to meet Quentin's tender gaze. "I know Michelle wanted you. Hell, every woman wants you. You are perfect."

He snorted.

"No, you are, Quentin. You truly are." Holly gnawed her lip as she tried to find the words to make him understand. "I forgave her because I understood that need to touch you, to be with you. But I couldn't forgive *you* because you crushed my heart. I thought you betrayed all I held dear. It was never that I trusted her over you. It was that I couldn't trust myself anymore." Reaching up, she trailed her fingertips over the chiseled planes of his face. "I kept you at a distance because to let you close was to expose myself to that kind of hurt again, and I couldn't bear to go through another heartache. There are always going to be women throwing themselves at you."

"I'm going on record as saying Beau and Michelle were duplicitous assholes with evil intent. He may never have physically hurt you until the night of the stabbing, but he was a master manipulator. Michelle was his perfect co-conspirator." He captured her hand and kissed the pad of her fingers. "What he did was mental and verbal abuse, Hol."

"I know that now, and yet, old habits die hard, ya know?"

"I'm not perfect. I'm far from it. I'm stubborn, and I take great delight in teasing you to anger."

"Now that you mention it, why do you do that?"

His smile bloomed fast and wide, showing a great expanse of straight, white teeth. "The color in your cheeks. The fiery look in your eyes. All that passion coming to life. It's erotic as hell, love. Whenever you turn into my prickly pear, I'm reminded of all the times we made love while we were together." He lowered his mouth to within an inch of hers. His breath mingled with hers. "You were wild, Hol. You were always up for anything. To this day, I've never known anyone as giving or responsive, anyone as sexy as you."

Holly closed the slight distance between them. When his lips opened under hers, she sighed her pleasure at the contact. And when his tongue zipped along the edge of hers, her sigh turned to a throaty moan.

Quentin. It was always Quentin. Even in her marriage bed, the ghost of him lingered. Maybe Beau knew it. If he had sensed her reserve, maybe she was the blame for her own trials and tribulations. Maybe he understood she would never love him as fully or completely as she'd once loved Quentin, how she would always love Quentin. He was the blood pulsing in her veins.

"I love you," she whispered. "I've always loved you, Quentin. I can't say it enough, and I'll spend the rest of my life apologizing for my mistakes."

"No, you won't. The past is done, Hol. We only go forward from here, okay?"

"Or backward."

He lifted his dark head in question.

"You said you had to go back to save me. How does that work?"

"I'm not exactly sure. All I do know is that I am to find an artifact known as the Cheirotonia Scroll, which coincidentally, is the same object your father needs. That's why this mission for your dad was a no-brainer from the get-go. Future me said that once I touch it, I will know what to do. It would take me back to a pivotal point in my life."

"I wonder why you chose that point in time?"

The look of disbelief he shot her was comical in nature. He shook his head and tucked a lock of her wayward hair behind her ear. "I couldn't let you be murdered."

"No, that's not what I mean. Why not go back to before Michelle pulled her stunt? Why not go back to the beginning and write a note to the two of us, explaining what was to happen?"

Quentin seemed to think about this for a few moments. "Because Michelle would find another time or place to attempt to break us up. And about the note, would you really believe it wasn't a prank?"

"Both good points."

"Hol…" He paused and swallowed. "What if I went back and

made sure we never got together?"

Holly's lungs lost their ability to function, and she found it impossible to breathe. The pain in her chest was crushing, and she thought she must be having heart failure. She had been lonely for a long time, and now, when she believed a relationship with the single most important person in her world was on the horizon, he stood in front of her, telling her he was thinking about trashing it all.

She was unable to articulate her grief, and yet he saw through her immediately.

"You are taking this wrong, love. I've had years to think about this. It isn't a rejection of us. It's to save your life." He placed a hand on either side of her face to gain her undivided attention. "If there is no us, Michelle won't try to destroy our relationship. You won't go running off with Beau, and no one will ever know what we are. They won't fear you or try to kill you for being as powerful as you are."

"But to never have met you, Quentin? To never have spent that year and a half in your arms and to never have a future with you would make my life colorless."

"Oh, Hol." The sweet reverence in his voice, the understanding, all cut her to the quick. At the same time, the strong emotion in his eyes made her heart beat fast. Made her want to lose herself in his embrace.

"I've been alone for too many years." She waved a hand when he would have spoken. "Oh, I know you were always there, waiting for me to come to my senses, but all that time I was unable to trust myself. All I want is you. Anywhere you are is where I belong, Quentin. Please don't wish that away. *Please.*"

The conflicted emotions he was experiencing were reflected in his tortured eyes. Holly reached up to smooth his furrowed brow. "I have to believe it will all be all right in the end. Without you, what is there?"

"My question exactly." His mouth claimed hers in a possessive move that left her breathless. "No more talking. Let's exist in the here and now, love."

Her answer was to shift and draw him down on top of her.

CHAPTER 12

Quentin burrowed his fingers in Holly's splayed out hair, cradling her head to memorize her features. Not that he needed to. From years of shadowing her, of playing bodyguard from afar and from up close, he knew every curve of her face, the contours and tones of her skin, the exact number of the smatter of freckles on her nose—thirteen.

He wanted to speak. To assure her of his love and promise her forever, but he knew he couldn't. Life didn't work that way. But he could show her. He could worship her body as he had done in his secret fantasies for years on end.

With the utmost tenderness, he brushed her nose with his then kissed the tip. The large, luminous eyes she turned his way told him all he needed to know. Words weren't necessary with their connection. Not anymore. Maybe they never had been. The outpouring of love, on both sides, was visible to each of them and probably to any who happened to witness an exchanged glance.

How had he ever been idiot enough to believe she ever loved Beau? She couldn't have, not the way she was looking at him this exact moment.

Emotion sat thick in his throat. This magnificent woman, fearless in all but love, was his. Everyone had their kryptonite. Holly was his; her fear of being hurt was hers. It all came to him in that moment. Like an epiphany.

"What are you thinking about, Quentin?" she asked softly.

"I'm trying to decide where to start. Which delectable part of your body needs my attention first."

Her naughty smile bloomed and took over her entire face. "Are you fishing for suggestions? I have a number of ideas."

His answering grin had to be as wide as hers. "I'll bet you do, love. But I've got this."

"Then get to getting. My body needs reminding of what you can do."

Ever so slowly, as to not break eye contact until the last possible second, he lowered his head. Their kiss was soul shattering. Long and drugging, yet it pulled him back to when they were young and passionate. When he drew away, they both struggled to draw a breath.

"How's that for a start?" he murmured.

"Fuck, yeah! *Achoo!*"

Neither acknowledged the rat-a-tat-tat at the window. They were drunk on each other, on a kiss that would wreck lesser mortals.

"I think it's about time I paid attention to this spot here." Quentin nuzzled the sensitive area beneath her ear and suppressed his smile when he heard her breathless giggle.

She ran a finger down the valley between her breasts. "What about this spot? I'm sure it's been neglected."

"Don't rush me, woman. I plan to taste every square inch of you."

"My apologies."

As she positioned her hand to snap away their clothes, he covered her hand with his. "No. I'm doing this the old-fashioned way."

A simple roll and shift of their positions had her settled atop him with her firm, shapely thighs straddling his hips. The heat of her core came through their clothing, and he smiled with satisfaction.

She leaned over him, and the silky strands of her dark hair brushed his face and clung to his stubble.

"I should have shaved."

"No." Her nails raked his two-day beard growth. "I like it."

The light teal shirt she had on blocked his view of her full breasts.

"You're wearing too many clothes, love. Let's start by removing this shirt."

Even anticipating Holly's impatience, Quentin unfastened one closure after another in his own good time. With each button he released, he trailed his fingertips over the creamy skin behind the cotton material and followed it with a light lick.

"Quentin, you're killing me! Remove the stinking shirt already."

"Uh, uh, uh." He wagged a finger in her face although his attention was still caught by the outline of the breasts about to be exposed. "I haven't been able to touch you the way I've wanted for seven years. We're not rushing this. It takes finesse. You'll remember that I like to take my time to unwrap my packages and prolong the anticipation." He met her frustrated gaze. "Nothing good ever comes easy, Hol."

Her face scrunched, and she huffed out a hard breath. "I think we can agree this hasn't been easy. And the anticipation you're talking about? Yeah, that's had a lot of years to build." Scooting back and resting on her thighs, she took the choice out of his hands and ripped her shirt open, dislodging the remaining buttons. "All that flirting and those teasing tastes of what we had? You're the master of the long, slow burn."

Holly squirmed, and his dick strained against his zipper. Without conscious thought, his hands found her hips and he rubbed himself between her thighs. "Maybe you have a point."

"I want to have your point," she teased. With a raised brow, she lifted her hands and snapped her fingers, zapping away their remaining clothing.

He inhaled sharply. The sight of her—hair tumbled around her shoulders, brushing the peaks of her breasts, the flat abdomen, and full hips—had his cock standing at attention.

When she stroked him, he had to count backwards from twenty in order to not shame himself. So much for leisurely lovemaking. If he didn't find a way to draw it out, it was going to be wham-bam-thank-you-ma'am.

"You need to keep your hands to yourself if you want me to last more than two minutes, Hol."

"I don't care if you last thirty seconds as long as I get off."

In another quick shifting of their positions, he had her flat on her back with her hands locked above her head. Transferring both her wrists into his one hand, he rubbed the pad of his thumb over her lower lip. "What kind of boyfriend would I be if I only gave you thirty seconds of lovemaking?"

"Quentin, if you don't do me right now, I'm going to lose my shi—"

He took her mouth in a frenzy of passion. Their tongues battled for supremacy as she twisted to pull free of his grasp. All she succeeded in doing was to arouse him to the point of insanity.

"Easy, love. My control is hanging by a very thin thread."

She bucked against him and bit his lower lip. "Good."

"I don't want to hurt you."

"You never would. Now stop talking and put that thing in me, will ya?"

"You are the most impatient—"

She cut him off with another love bite. Her tone turned coaxing. "Quentin, please."

He released her wrist and cupped her breasts. Dropping his head, he ran his tongue over the hardened tip, then drew it between his teeth to nip her in return. When she gasped, he tugged a little harder. The throaty moan drove him to duplicate the maneuver on her other breast.

Holly wound fingers and thumbs into his hair, pushing him downward.

He smiled against her belly then skimmed his teeth along on the underside of her bellybutton. The quiver of her stomach muscles told him how much she liked it, and he did it again.

With his right index finger, he dipped into the wetness at her opening and used it as a lubricant to swirl up and down her folds. Her hips rose from the bed, driving her toward his mouth. Because he was feeling inclined to feast on her, he wrapped his arms around her legs, stretching her then buried his face against her.

She tasted like the nectar of the gods, as sweet as honey and as spicy as cinnamon. Her orgasmic cries echoed about the room, and still, he worked her with his fingers and tongue. Plunging, tasting, readying her for him.

"Please," she begged. "Quentin, please!" she screamed as she crested the second release.

He sat back on his heels and looked down at her writhing body. Her hands clenched the thick folds of the comforter while her legs trembled with her need. But it was her eyes, like the darkest, stormiest sea, that drew him.

Never breaking eye contact, he guided himself to her slick opening. Her eyes widened a fraction as he filled her. When her lids fluttered shut, the beast within him protested. With a fierceness that surprised him, he growled, "Never shut me out again. Look at me, Holly." He thrust hard. "Look at me."

Her gaze never left his as he moved—at first in long, drawn out strokes, then in with faster, forceful thrusts.

"I see you, Quentin. I've always seen you."

He captured her joyful cry with a kiss as the waves of her release crashed over her. Without pausing, he continued to thrust, and with each drive of his hips, he lavished her with words of love.

It wasn't until she grabbed his face and said the words "I love you, Quentin" that he allowed himself to let go.

When they were snuggled together under the quilt, her ear over his rapidly thudding heart, he sighed his contentment. This was what he missed. Their closeness. The shared emotion. The oneness.

As he was dosing off, she spoke. "Drew Parker asked me out a few years back."

His eyes snapped open, and he lifted his head to stare down at her. The mischievous expression on her face told him he wasn't catching a nap anytime in the near future. "The dweeby, blond-haired guy?"

"He was scholarly, but yes. He never showed up for our date."

"Hmm. Imagine that." He thunked his head back against the pillow and struggled not to laugh. He suspected she was onto him, but he'd wait until the conversation played out.

"Coincidentally, you showed up at the coffeehouse that same night."

Yes, she definitely suspected him of a nefarious trick. "It shouldn't be considered a coincidence, love."

"No?"

"No."

"Did you scare him away, Quentin?"

Because she seemed more curious than annoyed, he confessed. "Not at all. I firmly suggested he find another woman to date."

"And?"

"And I may have flattened the tires of his drab little Honda Civic."

"I see." She bit her lip and cast her eyes downward, but not before he saw the laughing twinkle. "How many men did you make that same suggestion to?"

"Maybe three or four."

"That's not a lot."

"A month, for seven years."

Her laughter got the better of her, and Quentin delighted in the sound.

"I'm not even going to attempt the math on that one," she said.

He rolled her over and settled himself between her waiting thighs. "Roughly between two-hundred-seventy to three-hundred-thirty."

"Get out of here! There aren't even that many men in our hometown." In her astonishment, she pushed at him to sit up.

Leaning on one arm, he trailed a finger down the slope of her exposed breast and shot her a wicked look from beneath his lashes. "Okay, maybe I had to reinforce the suggestion a few times with the same guys. And maybe a portion of the three-hundred-thirty were only men trying to get an eyeful of your charms."

"That makes more sense." She flicked his forehead. "But let me get this straight. You got to sleep around, and I was stuck with a vibrator, using old memories of you and me?"

That got his full attention. "I'm having a hard time visualizing that. How about you show me—"

Holly slapped a hand over his mouth. "Oh, hush."

He lightly kissed her palm. "I didn't sleep around, Hol. Not after you were free."

When his seriousness sunk in, Holly's eyes nearly bugged out of her head. "Don't tell me you went seven years without sex!"

Quentin watched her with studied patience and a hint of a smile.

"How... what... what did you do for...?" Formulating a sentence was difficult in her shock.

"I did what you did."

"A vibrator and mental images of you?"

Unbidden, laughter bubbled up and out. "Close. My hand and mental images of you."

"You say the sweetest things. But admit it, you envisioned a threesome on occasion, didn't you?"

"I'll never tell."

"Not even if I do this?" She ran a finger the length of his dick.

It stirred to life under her touch, and he decided he could spend the rest of his natural born days in bed with her, having her tease him this way. "I'm not sure. You can keep that up, and we'll see what happens in the end."

Even as she laughed, she wrapped her hand around him and slowly stroked. "You're going to fold like a cheap napkin."

"More than likely. Keep doing what you're doing and see how fast that happens."

CHAPTER 13

*O*h, look! Chapter 13 has been eliminated. Surprise, surprise.

IN ALL SERIOUSNESS, I almost added it to throw you for a loop. But then I thought that tempting fate was for fools. Superstitious? Me? You betcha!

P.S. HAVE you added Long Lost Magic to your TBR list yet? Alastair's story is sure to delight!

CHAPTER 14

Quentin found it difficult to keep his hands to himself, but they finally managed to get a shower. Eventually, they sought out Nash, who was lingering poolside.

"About time you two showed up. I already grabbed breakfast, in case either of you cared that I was starving." Nash checked his watch. "Actually, now that it's time for lunch, do you want to find a café and make plans?"

"You only ever think of your stomach, brother."

"I think of you too, sister. Otherwise, I wouldn't be here trying to save you and your boyfriend's butts from the Council."

Holly leaned over and kissed her brother's cheek. "Thank you, Nash."

"Let's get to work. Our time is limited."

Quentin couldn't agree more. If they didn't get in and out of Greece quickly, they were likely to attract the unwanted attentions of Victor Salinger.

They settled on a small restaurant only a half-mile walk from the hotel. Nash mumbled a spell that muted their voices and confused anyone who might overhear their conversation. Quentin committed the words to memory for future use. One never knew when it might come in handy.

Holly was the first to speak. "Let's get down to business."

Nash held up a hand. "After I order."

"Your stomach is a bottomless pit, brother."

"Your point?"

"Can we shelve the argument, kids?" Quentin picked up his own menu and winked at Holly. "I have to admit to being hungry too."

After their orders were placed, Holly brought up the subject of Selene. "Obviously, any romance between her and Quentin is off the table. That leaves you, Nash. But more importantly, we need to find a way to get through the wards. Father told me that the National Museum is the Witches' Council stronghold for this half of Europe. It's going to be a bear to break through their magic."

"Maybe not," Quentin said thoughtfully.

Nash and Holly faced him.

"Nash, you're already a Council member in America. Wouldn't you already have clearance for this branch? If so, it would be a simple glamour spell to make you look like me. I think we could fool Selene enough for you to get in good with her."

"But how does that get you into the vault?" Nash asked.

Quentin grinned. "I glamour myself to look like you, and we walk in together. With the two of us side by side, no one will know who the wards opened for. That gets me past the initial security. Selene would latch onto you because she believes you, as me, would be after the scroll."

Holly leaned forward. "And me?"

"You go home and wait for us."

"Not going to happen."

Quentin sighed. "I had to try."

"I could cloak myself and enter with you both."

"Wouldn't work," Nash said and took a sip of wine. He gestured to their approaching server, and they all waited for the food to be placed on the table before they resumed their conversation.

"Why not?"

"The Council has cameras that pick up heat signatures. That means, even if you were invisible to the naked eye, you would still be detectable by a thermal camera."

"Then I go in with you as myself."

Both men groaned.

"What?"

"Hol, you…" When any reasonable excuse dried up, Quentin looked to Nash for assistance.

"You are a volcano waiting to blow, sister. It's not a good idea if you go with us." Before the protest left her lips, he added, "Besides, I doubt the Council would allow you through the doors."

"Why not?"

Nash gave a nonchalant shrug. "You are a Thorne. Not just any Thorne, but one of the most volatile of the lot."

"How do they know that?"

The hurt look on her face tugged at Quentin's heartstrings. He reached across and gripped her fingers. "I'm sure they keep tabs on all of you."

"They do," Nash confirmed then shoveled in a mouthful of bread dipped in taramasalata.

Quentin wanted to shove more than the appetizer into that arrogant shit's pie hole, but his size-thirteen foot sticking out of Nash's face might raise questions.

"They can't keep me from visiting the museum. It's open to the public."

With his inconsiderate words, Nash had drawn a line in the sand for Holly. Now, she was more determined than ever to enter that damned building, and there was no way in hell Quentin could sway her once her mind was set.

Rubbing the spot above his right eyebrow where a dull throbbing had begun, he tried to think through various scenarios that might appease Holly. He found it difficult to come up with a single one.

Setting down his eating utensils with great care, Nash folded his hands atop the table and sighed deeply. "Holly, pay attention and try to wrap your brain around this one. You will only get Quentin caught or possibly injured if you insist on participating in the retrieval of the scroll. You are far too impulsive to make this a successful mission."

Other than a slight increase to the speed of her breathing, Holly betrayed no outward sign she was upset. Her eyes remained locked on her brother, and Quentin held his breath, waiting for the explosion. A quick glance at their water glasses showed her struggle to keep her temper in check. Only a few bubbles made it to the surface.

"Hol—"

"It's okay, Quentin. I'm used to it." Slowly, as if she were a hundred years old, she gained her feet and laid down her napkin. "My *family* all seem to think I'm useless."

Alarm flashed in Nash's eyes. "That's not what I said. I—"

"I find I'm not hungry. I'll leave you to plan your *mission*."

Hating the dull, defeated look in her eyes, Quentin snagged her wrist before she could run off. "Hol—"

She shook her head and stared down at the point where his fingers were wrapped around the fine bones of her wrist. "Let me go. Please. I need air."

"I'll take you back to the hotel."

"It's only a few blocks, and the street is a main thoroughfare. I'm not likely to be abducted in broad daylight. Seriously, you and Nash need to figure out how this is going to work."

"Don't do anything cra—" Quentin stopped himself when her furious gaze snapped to his. "I didn't mean that."

The water in the glasses started at a slow boil.

"Sure you did." Holly jerked free of his hold. "But don't worry. I'll be the perfect little angel and wait for you both to do the heavy lifting. I wouldn't want to screw anything up for you."

"You're being overly dramatic, sister."

Without warning, Holly grabbed Nash's ear and yanked. "And you're being an *asshole*," she spat. She released him with a smug laugh and sailed out the door of the restaurant.

"I should follow her."

"Unless you have a hunch something bad is about to happen to her, leave her be, Quentin. We have things to discuss. I want to know how it was possible for her to swear that emphatically and not bring the entire avian population down on our heads?"

From his vantage point, Quentin could see Holly stalking down the sidewalk toward the hotel. Passersby must've sensed the violence brewing beneath the surface because they all moved out of her way. He turned a mocking smile on her brother. "That's her secret to share if she chooses."

"She has you pussy-whipped."

"I'm not ashamed to admit it."

Nash sat back with wine in hand to study him. "No, I don't suppose you are. I find I like you."

The words were eerily similar to Alastair's a few days earlier, and Quentin found himself chuckling. Nash would rather gouge out his own eardrums than hear he and his father were twins born forty years apart.

"What's so funny?"

"Private joke. Let's come up with a few alternative courses of action for tonight. I imagine we may have to play a few things by ear, and I don't want any surprises. Also, I need to check on Holly before we go tonight."

"Tonight?"

"It has to be tonight."

"Is it a coincidence that there's a gala at the museum this very night?"

"No."

"Good to know."

ONCE HOLLY WAS out of sight of the restaurant, she willfully ignored her quasi-promise to go back to the hotel and caught a cab to head to the National Archaeological Museum. After she arrived, she stood at the base of the steps and stared at the imposing building with its large stone columns.

Was she being an impulsive fool by coming here to scope out the place? Or was she really only here to scope out the competition? What was it about Selene that had her this disturbed?

Holly spun to leave when the clicking of heels on pavement captured her attention. Of *course* it had to be the woman who was quickly turning into her nemesis. Selene strode forward with all the grace and confidence of a lioness. Each step was perfectly placed to move her forward, and the purpose behind her strut left Holly in little doubt that the woman was as fierce as the cat to which she'd been compared.

Watching Selene coming toward her, Holly's heart sunk to her toes. This gorgeous creature was the perfect match for Quentin's stunning good looks.

"We meet twice in less than twenty-four hours. Is this a coincidence, Ms. Thorne?"

"Would you believe me if I said yes?"

Amusement brightened the dark mocha of Selene's eyes. "I believe I would." She studied Holly for an extra moment or two. "Would you like to join me for coffee? There is a café off the gardens."

Despite feeling gauche and very much like a country bumpkin next to this sophisticated woman, Holly said, "I believe I would."

"Splendid. My name is Selene Barringer."

"You're English."

Selene's brows shot up.

"Last night, I didn't get to talk to you at length. I missed the accent." Holly fluttered a hand up and down. "I thought you were Greek or Italian. Plus, there is that exotic beauty thing you've got going on."

Lips twitching, Selene nodded. "Thank you. My mother was Greek, my father was English. If you'd care to follow me, I'll lead the way to the café."

"How is it that you know who I am, Ms. Barringer?"

"It's my business to know things. The Thornes are infamous in the witch community. Seeing one of you outside the United States is like seeing a zebra in London's Trafalgar Square."

"A complete oddity."

"Exactly."

Speaking of oddities, as much as she wanted to hate Selene, Holly found herself admiring the woman walking next to her. The quick wit and graciousness were appealing.

After they were seated and waiting for a server to deliver their drinks, the two of them made small talk. Unease coated Holly's veins when Selene turned the conversation to Quentin.

"The man who was with you last night, Quentin Buchanan; how well do you know him?"

"I thought it was your business to know all about the Thornes?" Holly quipped before taking a sip of her steaming coffee.

"Touché. But then, he isn't a Thorne, is he?"

With a shrug, Holly answered, "We've known each other all our adult lives. For a brief while, we were an item."

Selene frowned as she ran a well-manicured finger around the rim of the ceramic cup. "For a brief while? Last night, he stated you were his girlfriend. Is that not true?"

"There are things we are working through."

Surprisingly, sympathy flashed across the other woman's face, and Holly found her stomach flip-flopping at the sight.

"Holly—may I call you Holly?—why are you here in Athens?"

"I don't understand what you mean." Holly's hand crept up to the tanzanite necklace.

"You're too smart for games. We both know you are in Athens for more than a vacation. Thornes don't venture far from their home. Call it a security blanket. Again I ask, why are you here?"

"Why do *you* think I'm here, Selene?"

"What the devil do you think you are doing engaging Selene?" Alastair's voice boomed loudly in her head, and Holly nearly winced.

A small smile twisted Selene's luscious mouth. "I think you are here for an ancient artifact. The rumor is that your family seems to be collecting items for your father."

"It's true," she said, waiting for the explosion through the telepathic connection to her father. It was easy to predict his ire.

"For the love of all that is holy!"

And there it was.

Struggling with laughter, Holly bit her lip.

"I'm surprised by your honesty," Selene told her.

"She isn't the only one."

Again, Holly shrugged. "What is the point of lying? I'm terrible at it, and I'm sure you've already been alerted by the Witches' Council."

"So, you *do* need the Cheirotonia Scroll."

"The what?"

Selene seemed taken aback by Holly's question. "The Cheirotonia Scroll. I was informed it would be your target."

"You were informed wrong."

"Tell her you are after the Magic Sphere of Helios on display at the Acropolis Museum."

"I'm after the Magic Sphere of Helios. I believe it is on display at the Acropolis Museum?"

Selene's dark eyes lost any semblance of friendliness. "You're lying."

"I thought we established that I'm a terrible liar."

"I've been told Alastair Thorne is trying to resurrect Aurora Fennell-Thorne. He'll need the scroll to do it."

"Actually, he doesn't. The last item on his list is the Helios. It's supposed to work in conjunction with the other artifacts he's collected. Or at least according to our source, it will."

"Your source?"

"Don't you dare tell her Isis is your source, Holly Anne!"

"Yes. Well, it's more like my father's source. I don't have a source. Never spoken to a source really." Holly found herself becoming warm under Selene's hawk-like scrutiny. Babbling was a direct result of the lies crossing Holly's lips. She hadn't been kidding when she said she was a terrible liar. Or she was when her father's voice was thundering in her brain.

Holly bolted to her feet. "Uh, I have to go. Quentin will be wondering where I am by now. He was going to meet me at the Acropolis Museum."

Selene rose in one graceful motion. "We are having a fundraising gala here tonight. You may have noticed the banner and the red carpet at the front of the building. I'd be delighted if you and Mr. Buchanan would be my guests tonight."

How was she expected to decline?

"You're not. Accept her invitation with dignity and depart at once."

"Sure. I accept. Uh, is there a will-call?"

"Will-call?"

"A ticket window."

Selene's amusement was back. "I'll be sure to have an attendant keep an eye out for you and your delightful companion." Her discerning gaze ran the length of Holly's form, taking in her capri pants, V-neck shirt, and sandals. "The gala is black-tie. Would you like me to recommend a boutique?"

"No need. I've got it covered. I'm all about the black-tie parties."

Alastair groaned in her head.

"Until tonight, Holly Thorne."

"Actually, it's Hill. I... never mind, I was planning to change it anyway." What the hell was wrong with her? She practically caved under the pressure.

"You did well, child. Now do me a favor and get the hell out of there."

"Well, at least there is one good thing about telepathy—no sneezing when we cuss."

Alastair's laughter echoed through the connection. *"You're incorrigible, dear girl. Completely incorrigible."*

CHAPTER 15

*A*lastair's arrival heralded no surprise for Holly. His expression was one of long-suffering when he asked, "What were you thinking, child?"

"Obviously, she wasn't," Nash snapped.

Quentin's quiet watchfulness was truly the thing that made her the most nervous. Their new bond was tentative at best, and she had no desire to destroy it. She ignored her father and brother to cross to Quentin's side. "Are you mad at me?"

"No, love. We were the idiots who excluded you and pissed you off. I should've anticipated you'd run off to confront Selene."

"That wasn't my intent."

He raised a questioning brow.

"Well, not entirely," she amended. "I thought if I could get the layout of the museum, I could help get a jump on your mission tonight."

"Uh, huh. Where is the copy of the layout?"

"I never made it past the café."

Quentin's grin eased the tightness in her chest. "It's always about food with this family."

"The baklava was to die for."

When he lightly ran a finger down her nose, Holly knew he'd forgiven her impulsiveness.

"I'm hurt you didn't bring me any." He leaned down to drop a light kiss on her smiling mouth. "It's a good thing there is a PDF of the layout available on the museum website."

"Seriously?"

"Seriously."

"That's like giving a roadmap to all the thieves out there."

"Like us?" he laughed.

"We aren't thieves. We are procurers of magical artifacts."

Again, Quentin laughed. "Never change, Hol. You are perfect exactly the way you are."

Tears burned her eyes as she stared up at him. He meant the words he'd spoken. Truly meant that, in his eyes, she was perfect.

"Pussy-whipped." Nash sandwiched his insult between coughs.

"I'm going to blast him to the Arctic," she muttered.

"Not until after you retrieve the scroll. You're going to need him," Alastair warned.

"I thought Nash said you wanted us to abort the mission?" Holly asked.

Her father met her question with a wry look. "When have you ever done anything I demanded of you, child?"

Because he was right, Holly changed the subject. "Selene mentioned the gala tonight and invited us to attend." Her comment brought all the men up short.

"She invited us?" The disbelief in Nash's voice was obvious to one and all.

"Well, not you. She invited me and Quentin. I didn't ask about you because you work for the Council. I assumed you could get your own ticket." She bit her lip to stem her laugh. Nash's dismayed look was comical. With a dismissive wave of her hand, she faced Quentin. "We need to go to the Acropolis Museum, like right now."

At his confused look, she explained. "I sort of told Selene we were after an artifact from there."

"Ah, yes. Your dad said as much. But why do we need to go to the Acropolis?"

"Because I said I was supposed to meet you there. If Selene has people watching us, I don't want to be caught in a lie." She cast an uneasy glance around the room. "Did anyone think to ward these suites against scrying?"

"I put a spell in place for my room when I first arrived," Quentin assured her. "You?"

"I didn't think to," she confessed.

"I took care of that when I got here," Nash informed her. "I figured you were too distracted."

"Thank you." To Quentin, she asked, "Should we go?"

"Teleporting in such a busy city is foolish," Nash warned.

"It was my intent to hail a cab. Like I did today." She scowled her ire. "Stop treating me as if I was born yesterday."

In a move that surprised her, Nash stepped in and hugged her. "I made the assumption that you were not well-traveled or wise to the ways of the world, sister. I'm sorry. I should know you possess enough common sense to be useful to the cause. I was being an asshat." His sudden grin was a thing of beauty. "I absolutely love that I can swear and not call all the trash pandas on the continent."

"I don't know. I think you got the best of all of us. Summer has rodents. Mine isn't much better with birds. Our father has locusts. Raccoons are cute and cuddly."

"Unless they are rabid," Alastair deadpanned.

"Are you staying for the gala, Dad? It would set the Witches' Council on their collective ear."

"Your mother's health is failing, child. I don't wish to be away from her unless it's necessary. I came here today to warn you against becoming too friendly with Selene." With a sharp look in Quentin's direction, Alastair continued. "It's long been believed that she works for Victor Salinger."

"In case we should happen to encounter him, what does Victor look like?"

"Tall, maybe six-two or three. Clean shaven. Deep auburn hair and dark brown eyes. I suppose to the opposite sex he is considered extremely attractive. With his English accent, he even comes across as exceedingly charming, but he's dangerous, Holly. Never make the mistake of thinking that he has an ounce of humanity."

"English? Selene told me her father was English. Do you suppose there is a deeper connection there than the standard cohorts? I mean, Barringer and Salinger. Granted they are different names, but still coincidental that they both end in -inger, don't you think?"

Keeping his thoughtful eyes on her, Alastair turned his head slightly to address Nash. "Have you ever thought to check their family trees?"

"Other than Victor, no. You should know, if you don't already, he descends from the Goddess Serqet's line. He once had a half-sister, but she supposedly died at a young age."

"Supposedly?" Quentin asked.

"His father remarried when Victor was about ten. The marriage ended in divorce after the couple's young daughter disappeared. She was presumed dead."

"What happened to Barringer's ex-wife?"

"She changed her name and moved here to Greece. A few years later, she adopted a daughter. But the ex-wife and her adopted daughter were killed in a house fire six months after the adoption was finalized."

"And Selene's family history?" Alastair asked.

"We've never been able to dig anything up on her. The Council has her records on lockdown."

Alastair looked grim. "I've never been able to dig up anything on her either, which is unusual in itself. Normally, a simple scrying spell will allow me to dig into the past, but hers is blocked."

To Holly, this revelation was astounding. "You said she was linked to Victor. In what way? Lover, employee, spy, all of the above?"

"Never as a lover that we know of. She is simply his source of information. She feeds him tidbits about the Council business and on occasion, an artifact or two winds up in his hands."

"Is it possible his sister never really died? Who was the child that the ex-Mrs. Barringer adopted? Could it have been a ruse to get her own child away from a dangerous situation?"

"But the body of a girl was found in the burned-out ruins of her home," Nash informed her.

"I guess we'll never know unless we ask Selene herself," Holly said.

Quentin wrapped his arms around her from behind. "Not a good idea, Hol. You need to stay as far away from Selene and Victor as possible. I don't need the gray hairs that would come from you tangling with them."

"It's too late since I've accepted her invite for tonight."

His heavy sigh ruffled her hair.

"Don't worry, Quentin, I promise not to take unnecessary risks."

"I'd prefer you didn't take any risks, love."

"It's all going to work out, remember? You always get the scroll and save me."

"What did you say?" Alastair's sharp question startled them apart. "What do you mean he saves you? From what?"

Her hand found Quentin's, and she wove her fingers through his in unity. "That would be from the stabbing seven years ago."

She'd never seen her father shell-shocked before, but there he stood in a stunned stupor, staring at the two of them as if he'd just heard the world was ending and they only had ten more minutes to live. His face grayed.

"Dad?"

"The rumor is that the magic of the scroll can only be used one time in every hundred years," Alastair finally managed as he sat down heavily in a nearby armchair.

The impact of his words had Holly sinking down onto the leather sofa since her legs would no longer support her. Quentin could use the scroll to go back in time to save her, or he could hand it over to Alastair to save Aurora. There were no other options. And yet, if they'd truly been here before, Quentin always chose her over her mother.

Holly's eyes sought Quentin. He was as serious as she'd ever seen him as he addressed Alastair. "It's no contest, sir. I will always rescue Holly."

Alastair closed his eyes, expression resigned. "As you should, son. As you should."

"No!" Holly sprang to her feet and shoved past Quentin to kneel by her father's chair. "No, Daddy. He should help Mother. He said it himself; over three hundred times he's saved me, and nothing has changed. We still find ourselves in the same ugly time loop." The sensation of inevitability caught up to her, and she placed a hand on his knee. "Maybe I was never meant to survive that damned stabbing."

The swift surge of fury from Alastair charged the atmosphere around them. The air crackled with angry energy as he gripped her arms and shook her. "*Never* say that. Do you hear me? Never!"

Holly stared in shocked wonder at this side of her father. Not once had she seen him in such a rage. Part of her feared him in that moment. Her alarm must have shown because he released her arms to cup her face.

"I'm sorry, Sprite. Forgive me?"

Her father hadn't called her "Sprite" in what seemed like forever. All the emotions she'd suppressed over the years slammed into her. The hurt, anger, loneliness, and most importantly, the love, fought for supremacy. A harsh sob tore from her throat. Alastair gathered her close as she buried her face in his warm neck. She let loose all the buried pain and allowed her father to comfort her in a way she hadn't tolerated since she was a small child.

Inside, her tougher persona squirmed. These emotional outbursts were getting out of control, and yet, her tears refused to be stemmed. Perhaps it was because she hadn't cried in well over nine years. Not since the night she was tricked into believing Quentin had cheated. Now, it seemed as though she cried at the drop of a hat.

Somewhere, in the back of her subconscious, she was aware of Quentin and Nash exiting the room.

"It's okay. You're okay." Her father rocked her while she cried.

The raw, husky quality to his voice betrayed his own strong emotions.

When she could finally manage to speak, she drew back and stared up into his ravaged face. She imagined she looked far worse. "How do we bring her back?"

"I don't know. I truly don't know now."

"Can we summon Isis? She could tell us."

"We cannot ask her, child." He lovingly smoothed back her hair. "She would demand a sacrifice. What more does our family have to offer? Haven't I put everyone through enough at this point? Your sisters..." His mouth tightened into a firm line. "I think it's time we accept what was fated."

It was the crack in Alastair's voice that did it. It killed her to see him so wrecked. "No, Dad. I have no intention of accepting what is fated. I'm going to find another object to help her, or Quentin can find another to go back for me. But this isn't the end for either of us." She didn't tell him that she was for saving her mother at this point. Aurora and Alastair had been parted long enough, and for all the work that her father had put in to ensure the happiness of her sisters, he damned well deserved a happy ending himself.

"I know that look, my dear girl. You are up to no good."

Did his voice hold an underlying weariness?

"You know me too well. But I promise to take care with my schemes this time."

His mouth twisted in a semblance of a smile. "Fair enough." He rose and helped her to stand. "Glamour away your upset and get your behind to the Acropolis Museum before Selene realizes you lied."

"I suspect she already knows I lied since I suck at it, but yeah, I'll go do that now. Will you tell Quentin I'd like to speak to him before you head back home?"

"Certainly."

Holly clasped his large hand between both of hers and drew it to her cheek. "I love you, Dad. I always have, even when I was being a little shit."

"I love you, too. And I suspect you are enjoying cursing without consequence a bit too much," he said wryly. "Take care of yourself. If you don't, I'll blame Quentin. I know how much you love him and would hate to see him come to harm at my hand."

"Not fair!"

"I never claimed to be, Sprite. Not once."

He strode over to the bed and held out his hand, palm down. A blinding gold light filled the space between his palm and the comforter. Within seconds the light morphed into a brilliant red before it disappeared altogether.

On the bed was a sequined evening gown in the most breathtaking shade of sea foam green.

"Is that for me?"

"I doubt it will fit Quentin."

"Alastair Thorne has jokes! Who knew?" she teased.

"Adjust the length of the tanzanite necklace by about two inches for it to sit higher on your décolletage. I suggest a sweep of your hair to one side with a diamond clip. You'll find one there beside the dress."

"I've never had much call to dress up."

"I know. It's why I provided you with the basic tools. You can conjure your own shoes for comfort purposes. Silver Cinderella Slippers like the ones Stuart Weitzman designed would be the thing."

"How do you know about women's attire?"

A wolfish grin transformed his face. "Just because I'm on a diet, doesn't mean I can't look at the menu. I appreciate a beautiful woman as much as the next man."

"I'm so telling Mom."

His laughter could be heard long after he left her suite.

CHAPTER 16

*A*s Quentin absent-mindedly spoke with Nash, he mentally replayed the earlier scene in the bedroom. Alastair's devastation had been hard to witness. The choice between the love of his life or his daughter was a no-brainer. Aurora was in stasis, and even with the scroll, there existed a very real chance of failure if they tried to revive her. On the other hand, getting to Holly in time to save her from a fatal stabbing was not only possible, it was assured.

As the one tasked with retrieving the ancient artifact, Quentin would never be able to turn it over to Alastair if he refused to put Holly first.

He hadn't known the scroll could only be used once within a hundred-year time period. That was one little factoid Athena had failed to mention to him last night. Still, it was one that made no sense. Based on the Goddess's revelation, Quentin had returned over three-hundred times. There was no possible way those times were a hundred years apart. The math didn't add up. Could he find a way to summon Athena before tonight to discover the truth?

When Nash's words trailed off, Quentin glanced behind him. Alastair looked as serious and defeated as Quentin had ever seen him.

"I must return home to Rorie." No matter how casual he tried to be, Alastair failed to hide his pain. "Time is short."

"If there was any other way…" Quentin trailed off. Sympathetic drivel wasn't warranted.

"You do what you must, Quentin. We all know where our priorities lie. My daughter mentioned that she'd like to speak with you." Alastair turned his attention to his son. "Nash, I need a moment with you in private."

As Quentin moved to pass Alastair, the older man placed a hand on his arm.

"Thank you, Quentin. You've always had her best interests at heart. No one could love her more."

"That's the truth, sir. But you don't need to thank me. She's easy to love."

Nash snorted behind him. "Keep telling yourself that, you poor sap."

In a low tone that only Quentin could hear, Alastair said, "His time is almost at hand. You'll be able to needle him plenty."

"Oh, I look forward to it."

"As do I."

Quentin closed the connecting door between the suites to offer the privacy the others needed. The shimmering material of the new dress caught his eye, and he approached the bed.

Holly's gown for the gala.

She would be a vision once she slipped it on. She always was when she was formally dressed. Of course, he'd only ever seen her dressed up twice: prom and her wedding day.

"Gorgeous, isn't it?"

"Did you conjure it?"

"Alastair did."

"The man has excellent taste. I can't wait to see it on you."

"We should get going if we want to hit the Acropolis Museum before the gala tonight."

Misgivings swarmed him, and he closed the distance between them and tipped up her chin. "I think you should go home with your father, Hol. I get the feeling your mother is fading fast. You should be there to say your goodbyes."

Tears swam in her eyes. He followed the path of one lone tear as it escaped down her cheek. Before the droplet could drip from her chin, he wiped the moisture away with the pad of his thumb.

"I don't want you to have regrets, love."

"I won't because we aren't going to let her die."

His gut twisted in response to her words. "I'm not about to let you do anything foolish. You have to know that."

"You can't stop me, Quentin." She stood in front of him with her arms folded across her chest. A determined glint shone in her eyes. He knew that look. It was the look that said she intended to do what she wanted and damn the consequences.

The sudden desire to wring her neck was upon him. With a concerted effort, he dropped his arms to his sides and backed away. "Then go," he snapped. "Go make whatever impulsive, bullshit move you intend to, so the rest of us can get busy cleaning up your mess."

Her startled gasp echoed around the room. "You don't get to talk to me like that."

"Don't I? If not me, who, Holly? *Who?*" All the pent-up frustration he'd felt at being rejected time and again boiled up. All the fear for her—past, present, and future—ganged up and made him mental. For the first time in ages, he lost control of his magic. The air around them began to swirl and rock the knick-knacks on the wood surfaces of the furniture around them. The artwork on the wall rattled as the curtains flapped. "You are the most stubborn, spoiled-rotten brat I've ever encountered in my life. Without ever having the facts, you charge off without a care for your or anyone else's safety because you happen to feel like it."

"That's not true!"

"It absolutely is. It's always your way, no matter what. Well, I for one am tired of it."

She stormed to where he stood and used the heels of her hands to ineffectively shove his chest. "Then leave!"

"This is my damned room!"

"Then I'll leave," she snapped, pivoting on her foot to head for the main hallway.

"That's right, run away. That's what you do best; avoidance."

His long legs ate up the distance in half the time it took her. Using the flat of his hand, he slammed it against the wooden plane of the door. It didn't matter that five seconds ago he wanted her to get out of Greece for her own safety. The contrary side of his nature had decided to rear its ugly head and weigh in.

"You avoided having an honest adult conversation with me about Michelle for nine years. You refused to seek out your father and apologize for your childish insistence that Beau Hill was a prince among men. Goddess *forbid*, you admit Alastair was right about that piece of shit!"

"Stop it!"

"How many times have you been to see your mother in the last eighteen years, Holly? Never while we were dating. I know that much."

"Stop!"

"You know what I think? I think you only came to Athens to stop me from moving on. You never wanted me, but you certainly don't want anyone else to have me either."

Her hands balled into tight fists, and her voice shook when she denied his claim. "That's not true, Quentin. I've always wanted you. Always!" Her tears flowed faster. "I'm yours, and you're mine."

"Tell it to someone who believes it, sweetheart. I don't anymore, and I'm tired of being used."

"Is that what you think this morning was all about? Me using you?"

"Didn't it scratch your itch?" He didn't give two damns that he was being crude as he grabbed himself. "Wasn't this all you were after? What you tell me all women are after?"

As Quentin watched, Holly's fire petered out. "Yes. That was all I was after."

Before he could form a retort, she teleported.

"Shit!"

He ran for the connecting door and yanked it open. The Thorne men stood side-by-side, arms folded and grim expressions on their faces.

"You heard," Quentin stated flatly.

Nash snorted his disbelief at the asinine question. "How could we not?"

"Where would she go?"

"The place you practically taunted her *to* go," Alastair replied. "But then, I believe you already know that."

"Okay, this is embarrassing, but I don't know where you live."

A slip of paper appeared in Alastair's hand. "Here."

A glance down showed the longitude and latitude of a specific location. "Is this the center of a volcano?"

Alastair's lips compressed, whether to hold back a bark of laughter or a healthy curse word, Quentin wasn't sure.

"For the record, I have no idea where all that rage came from a minute ago." Shitty as far as apologies go, but it was all he could manage.

"I do. Quite frankly, I'm surprised you lasted as long as you have. That location is my home. I'll call ahead and have Alfred admit you to the house."

"I thought you were heading that way?" Nash asked his father.

"Do I strike you as an idiot, son? I'm not stepping foot in that house until these two have had it out."

"Good plan," Nash agreed. He held out his palm, and an amber light spiraled up into the shape of a bottle. "Let's have a drink while we wait."

"I see the label says Glenfiddich. Good choice, but if that isn't at least a forty-year-old single malt scotch, don't bother pouring me any."

"Pfft! As if I didn't already know that. Conjure the glasses, Sperm Donor."

Alastair surprised Quentin when he produced three crystal tumblers and set them on the coffee table. "You have time, boy. Have a drink or two. You'll need the fortification for when you chase down my daughter."

"I'm not sure if I should. Chase her down, that is."

When the Thornes remained silent, as if to let him continue, Quentin explained. "If she's visiting Aurora, she's out of the way and less likely to get into trouble."

"A solid plan." Alastair raised his glass. "I'll toast to keeping Holly out of trouble any day of the week."

Nash shook his head and gazed down into the tumbler of amber liquid he held. "I don't think either of you are allowing her the right to choose her path."

"I don't understand. Weren't you the one rushing here yesterday to keep her out of harm's way?" Quentin could freely admit to being confused. Nash's about-face boggled the mind.

"She did what neither of us has up to this point. She obtained invitations to the gala and ingratiated herself with Selene." He gave a nonchalant shrug and sipped his drink. "While I don't approve of her spontaneity, she came through in the end. She's done it with a lot less hysterics than you, I might add."

Nash wasn't wrong. Quentin *had* been overly emotional these last few days. His temper was balanced on a razor's edge and flared with the slightest provocation. Not normal for him in the least. He could only blame it on his current stress levels. The time had come for him to preempt a major catastrophe by obtaining and utilizing that damned scroll. The position he found himself in was impossible. If he went back to the moment of the stabbing, he would reset the cycle again. If he didn't... well, he couldn't wrap his brain around that consequence.

The pinging of Nash's phone paused their conversation. Based on the sour expression Holly's brother made, the news wasn't ideal.

"Victor Salinger is in Athens."

Father and son shared a speaking glance.

"Bringing Holly back is out of the question," Quentin informed them.

"I still think she would be useful," Nash argued.

Alastair downed his drink in one smooth motion. "This is a blasted mess."

HOLLY PERCHED on the edge of her mother's sickbed and picked up her emaciated hand.

"Hey, Mom." She swallowed hard. "It's me. Holly."

Because looking at Aurora's gaunt face caused the acid to churn in Holly's gut, she studied the veins on the back of her mother's hand. With one fingertip she traced a blue line.

"I know I haven't been around to visit much, but I'm here now. Although I'm not sure if I'll be coming again after today." She tried to rub warmth back into the cold hand sandwiched between hers. "It's my hope that Quentin will use the scroll to revive you this time around. If he does that, I…"

What could she say? That she'd be trading her life for her mother's? No parent wanted to hear that.

"You'd like him, Mom. Quentin is amazing. I mean, not today, because I'm a little pissed at him if I'm being truthful, but most days he is."

With the back of her wrist, she swiped at the salty moisture filling her eyes.

"He's said some harsh truths lately. Things that I didn't want to hear, but that I needed to, ya know? I've been such a fool for too long."

Holly pressed the heels of her hands to her eye sockets.

"I wasted all those years the two of us could've had together. Would've had, if it weren't for Beau and Michelle."

With a clearing of her throat, she said, "But you don't know them either. Maybe one day, when you and I meet up in the Otherworld, I'll tell you all about it. Right now, it's too exhausting, and I don't want to spend any more time thinking about those two evil twatwaffles."

Lifting her eyes from the hand she'd been stroking, Holly studied her mother's fragile features.

"I really need you to come back for Dad's sake, Mom. He's lonely without you. He won't say it, but I know. You probably do, too. He's here all the time when he isn't managing everyone's lives."

A light laugh escaped her.

"It's funny to think that he's been matchmaking for me and my sisters. Sisters I didn't know I had, by-the-by. That's another thing we need to discuss. I'm a little irritated that you never told me. I had to find out this past summer when my long-lost twin walked through the door of the restaurant downtown."

She smiled to take the sting from her words, as if her mother could see what was going on from wherever her spirit resided.

"I adore her. Summer. She's the better of the two of us. There isn't a person she doesn't care for, or an animal for that matter. You should see her familiar, Mom. He's a little thug squirrel who never shuts up."

Reaching forward, she smoothed a lock of her mother's lank, black hair.

"Winnie looks like you, but you probably already know that. She's gorgeous. Funny, too. Although she has nothing on Autumn when it comes to sarcasm. That chick is hilarious."

She bent and kissed her mother's petal-soft cheek.

"Thanks for giving me such an incredible family, Mom. Oh, and you'd be proud of Spring. She buried that asshat, Zhu Lin, with a nice little earthquake she conjured."

Holly cocked her head to the side.

"I didn't sneeze! I guess if I'm touching immediate family, I'm immune. That means there's life in you yet, Mom. Please, keep hanging in there until Dad can find a way to revive you. Please?"

With great care, she rearranged the already straight sheet. It was silly, but she needed to feel as if she'd done some small thing to make her mother comfortable.

"I have to go now. I'm attending a gala in Athens tonight, and I need to get back to smooth things over with Quentin. I have to make him understand how much I love him."

She sniffed in her self-misery.

"I need to make him believe that I see him as more than a pretty package." She smiled wryly. "It's not to say he isn't. He absolutely is. Gorgeous as I've never seen before or probably ever will again. I don't know what he sees in me, Mom. I truly don't. He could have anyone he wants."

"But he wants you."

Holly spun around so fast she nearly wrenched her back. Lounging in the doorway with the casual grace he pulled off all too well, was Quentin. He uncrossed his arms and stood straighter. Love glowed from his dark, bedroom eyes. Love intended only for her.

"He only *ever* wanted you, Hol."

Whatever uncertainty had held her frozen in place disappeared. She was off the bed and rushing into his embrace in less time than it took to blink.

"Oh, Quentin! I'm sorry. I seem to be saying it every hour on the hour lately, but I truly am."

"Me, too, love. More than you know. I don't know why the hell I exploded like that."

"You were long overdue. At every turn, I was letting you down. But it doesn't matter anymore. What are you doing here?"

He grinned, and she felt it down to her toes. "I had to follow my prickly pear, didn't I?"

She laughed and hugged him tighter. "I'm glad you are as stubborn as you are. Others might find that a fault, ya know. Personally, I think it's your best trait."

"Mmhmm. We'll see what you think in another fifty years after you've been subjected to that stubbornness on a daily basis."

"Want to meet my mom?" she asked hesitantly.

"I thought you'd never ask."

CHAPTER 17

"It's time to go, Hol."

"I can't believe you aren't trying to keep me from going to the gala."

"You can thank your brother. He said we—we being me and your dad—need to let you walk your own path."

"Thank you."

"Don't for one minute believe I don't hate it, because I absolutely do. But he's right. You're an intelligent adult."

"I'll let Dad's overseer know we are leaving and ask him to keep an eye on my mom until my father returns."

"Since this house is intimidating as hell, I'll wait for you here. I wouldn't want to break anything and have your dad on my ass."

Holly stretched up to kiss him then headed for the door.

After she left, Quentin turned to stare down at the woman on the bed.

"I'm sorry, Aurora. I wanted to be able to help you, but your daughter is my first priority." He clasped her hand in his. "But I promise you, as long as there is a breath still left in my body, I will always take care of her."

He gently placed her hand down by her side, turned toward the door, and stopped short. Surprise initially stole his voice when he saw the woman standing before him. Or *through* the woman standing before him.

"Aurora," he croaked as the hair on his neck rose to attention. In her ghostly form, she was beautiful in that eerie, holy-crap-there's-a-ghost-in-front-of-me sort of way.

She glided toward the bed and stared down at her failing body. "Tell Alastair it's time to let me go."

When he didn't answer, she faced him. He was stunned witless by how warm and encompassing her sudden smile was. "You'll do that for me, won't you, Quentin Buchanan?"

"I'll tell him, ma'am. But I can guarantee he won't listen. The man is obsessed."

"Tell him what happened to me wasn't his fault, but this continued quest he's on will be for naught." She stepped forward and raised her hand as if she wanted to touch him. With a slight shake of her head, she dropped her arm. "Thank you for loving my daughter. Let her know I heard her, and I'm proud of the woman she's become."

"She'll be back any second. Can you wait for her?"

"Even if she were here now, she wouldn't be able to see me."

"I don't understand."

"You are unique in your ability. You're what is called a Traveler, Quentin. As a Traveler, you have the ability to journey through time and space as long as you possess the proper tools. Because Travelers can navigate through different dimensions, it makes the veil thin enough for you to see those of us on the other side."

His brows slammed together as he stared in open-mouthed wonder. How had he never heard the term Traveler or known what one could do? For that matter, how had he never discovered he had the ability to see ghosts and time travel?

"I see that I've confused you." She laughed, and the sound was melodic in nature. Holly shared that same laugh when she was happy. It never failed to brighten his day.

"You have definitely confused me." He shot her a self-depreci-ating smile. "I can't believe this is even real."

"Alastair's son, Nash, will be able to help you discover more."

"The Cheirotonia Scroll isn't the only 'tool' that will allow me to go through time?"

Aurora winked. "Now you're getting it." She turned and cocked her head. "Holly is returning. We should probably say our goodbyes. Otherwise, she might think you're talking to yourself."

"Wonderful," he muttered.

"Take care of yourself, darling boy."

"Thank you… for shedding light on my, er, gift."

"It's entirely my pleasure. Have a care tonight."

"Do you see all in the Otherworld?"

"Enough. Be careful of Victor Salinger." And with that, she was gone. Her disappearing coincided with Holly sailing through the door.

"Did I hear you talking with someone?"

His gaze was drawn to Aurora's stasis-prone form. "I'm embar-rassed to admit, I held a similar conversation with your mother as you did earlier."

Holly placed a hand over his heart. Did she feel the rapid beat? He wasn't quite certain he was over his initial fright from seeing a ghost appear, even if that spirit was friendly in nature.

"I think it's sweet. I'm sure if she were here, my mother would appreciate it."

"We should get going." He wrapped her in a tight hug and visual-ized his hotel room. As his cells harnessed magic for their teleport, he cast one last glance in Aurora's direction. He'd pass on her last wish to Alastair. It was the least he could do.

WHILE HOLLY WENT to change her clothes, Quentin approached Alastair and Nash. "May I have a word with you both?"

"What's going on, son?"

"You're not going to believe this. Hell, I'm not sure I believe it and I was there."

Nash, always seemingly a step ahead of everyone, said, "Spit it out, Quentin. You only have a few minutes if you don't want Holly in on this."

"I saw the spirit of Aurora."

There was an audible inhalation of air by Alastair.

"Come again," Nash replied.

"I saw the spirit of Aurora when Holly left the room to tell your butler we were leaving. She spoke to me."

Alastair presented his back and stared from the large floor-to-ceiling window out over the darkening landscape. "What did she say?"

Did Quentin imagine he heard a tremble in the older man's deep voice? For sure there was a raw edge to the question.

"She wants you to let her go."

The reflection in the glass showed Alastair's overwhelming shock at the news. His eyes closed tightly, and his mouth firmed.

"Is that all?" Nash asked quietly.

"No. She said I was a Traveler, and that you might know more about that."

Nash shook his head in wonder. "Of course. I've come across the term in a couple of the older book collections I've explored, but I've never known an actual Traveler. I thought they were made up—similar to unicorns."

Quentin cast a worried glance at the eerily still Alastair. "Sir? Are you okay?"

Alastair gave a sharp nod but remained silent.

Allowing Alastair his privacy, Quentin turned his back and addressed Nash. "Do you think you could help me discover more about this whole Traveler thing?"

"Before tonight? Not likely. But from what I have read, there are magical artifacts that help you move through time and worlds."

"Worlds?" He asked sharply. He thought about the garden Athena had taken him to during their brief time together. "Aurora only said time and space."

"I could be wrong. It's been a while, and I don't know how accurate the translation of the text was."

"Is there a list of these artifacts? I mean, is it possible to utilize a different one to stop Beau and Michelle in order for Alastair to get what he needs to revive Aurora?"

Nash poured himself another dram of whiskey and held up the bottle. When Quentin waved away the offer, Nash said, "No list. I have a few items in storage that might be useful, but they're untested. Do you have time to chance it?"

"No." Quentin expelled a heavy sigh. Their time crunch didn't allow for other options. Joining Alastair at the window, he said, "She seems happy to be in the Otherworld, sir. She wanted me to tell you what happened wasn't your fault."

Alastair ran a hand over the lower half of his face, as if to hold back the words he longed to say. With a small nod of acknowledgment, he continued to stare into the distance.

"What can I do to help? Tell me and I'll do it."

"There's nothing you can do now, son." The gruff tone spoke of heartbreak. "But I thank you. You should get ready for the gala. You don't want to keep Holly waiting."

"I'm sorry."

The dark indigo eyes Alastair turned on him were three shades darker than his normal iris color and devoid of emotion. Without a doubt, the man was in pain.

"I know. It's all right." Alastair held up his hand to show a pinky ring with a bluish-purple stone. "Holly is wearing a tanzanite necklace to match my ring. This allows us to communicate telepathically. Make sure she doesn't take it off." He cleared the remaining emotion from his throat. "When you get to the museum, find an out-of-the-way room and snap pictures to send to me. I need a clear space in the event I need to teleport as backup."

"Will that be necessary?"

"I've already warned you about Victor Salinger. Don't underestimate him, boy."

"I'll do whatever you ask."

Holly entered the room, drawing their attention. Her beauty almost drove Quentin to his knees to pay homage. Her pale sea foam dress showed enough cleavage to make a man's mouth water, but preserved her modesty at the same time. The sequins reflected the light with every step she took toward him. The coppery tresses he adored were swept to one side to reveal the long, creamy column of her neck.

Quentin wanted nothing more than to usher her back into his room and lock the world away.

"You're not dressed yet?" Her eyes darted between the men. "Was there a change of plans?"

"No change, love. We were discussing information that came to light about my elemental magic."

"Like what?"

"I'll explain in the car on the way." Quentin faced Nash. "Did you arrange for a ride?"

"I did."

"Thank you. I'll be ready in ten minutes." To Holly, he said, "Keep your father company for a little bit." With a side glance toward Alastair, he leaned in to whisper, "He's worried. Try to distract him a bit, huh?"

Holly shifted her head for their lips to meet. After a soft, lingering kiss, she nodded.

CHAPTER 18

$\mathcal{T}$he museum gala was in full swing by the time their limo pulled up to the curb. Nash exited first, followed by Quentin and Holly. As they made their way up the stairs, she touched the stone at her throat.

"How's our connection, Dad?"

"Strong as ever, child."

"Don't drink all the scotch before we get back."

"I can conjure more."

She smiled as she dropped her hand to her side.

"The sperm donor talking in your ear?" Nash murmured in an aside.

"Yes. He intends to drink all your Glenfiddich."

Nash clasped her hand before he spoke. "That bastard."

With a light laugh, she squeezed his fingers. "I thought I was the only one getting off on swearing without an invasion of wildlife."

"I could get used to this. I should have our cousin Liz design amulets that keep us connected so we can swear like normal people."

"Goddess, no! Please!" Quentin cut in. "She'll be cussing people out left and right."

With a mock scowl, she pinched his arm. "Not funny."

"I'm not kidding. Your violent tendency to pinch and punch is bad enough."

"You poor baby." With a rub of his abused arm, she whispered suggestively, "Remind me to kiss it and make it better later tonight."

"Promises, promises."

Nash gave an exaggerated shudder. "Eww. I'm still within hearing distance."

They paused ten feet from the door. Holly reached up to straighten Nash's bow tie as a guise to address both men. "Are we all clear on the game plan? Quentin and I will occupy Selene, and you will search out the vault with the magical artifacts. Once you find the room, text Quentin. He can use the excuse of going to the restroom to meet you while I keep our hostess distracted."

"When I've made the switch with the fake parchment Alastair gave me, I'll text you. We'll meet by the entrance. If we get separated, teleport into the limo or—worst-case scenario—back to the hotel suite," Quentin reiterated from their earlier planning session.

Nash snagged her wrist before Holly could move away. "If Salinger approaches you, you get away from him asap, got it?"

"I won't take any unnecessary risks."

"That wasn't a yes, sister."

"It's all you'll get from me, Nash."

"You're such a stubborn little—"

Holly jerked her arm from his grasp before he could blast her with the word "bitch." With a wicked grin, she entwined her arm through Quentin's and directed them toward the main doors.

"… Biotch!"

"Nice substitution, brother. Personally, I was hoping for a cute little trash panda to cuddle. Oh! Maybe I could make one my familiar."

"Knock it off. We have a job to do," Quentin reminded them.

His warning was well-timed. Selene stood twenty feet inside the entrance, greeting guests and patrons of the museum. When she saw their group, she excused herself to head their way.

"I'm delighted you could make it." Grabbing Holly's hands, Selene air kissed each side of Holly's cheeks. "Welcome."

After she pulled away, she sized up Quentin. "I didn't realize you were so tall, Mr. Buchanan."

Wanting to move Selene's overly interested attention away from Quentin, Holly cleared her throat and dragged Nash forward. "This is my half-brother, Nash Thorne. He works for the American branch of the Witches' Council."

Selene's eyes slowly ran the entire length of Nash's tall, well-built frame. "A pleasure," she murmured, holding her hand out to him.

"The pleasure is all mine."

Her brother's sudden shift into a debonair playboy nearly threw Holly for a loop. She'd never seen him as anything but serious, surly, or sarcastic. "Crap! I threw up a little in my mouth."

The first to burst into genuine laughter was Selene. Her irises lightened by a shade as she gazed at Holly. "If you lived in Athens, we'd be the best of friends. I'm certain of it." Her attention was caught by someone beyond Holly's shoulder. All humor left her face, replaced by an impersonal mask. "If you'll excuse me, there's a guest I must speak with." As she moved to pass, she whispered, "The item you seek is in a small chamber off the north hall. I would wrap up my business as quickly as possible, if I were you."

Their eyes locked in a brief moment of understanding before she continued on her way.

As one, their group turned to watch her sashay her way toward an imposing auburn-haired figure surrounded by what could only be his security detail.

"Do you think they know how ridiculous they look wearing mirrored sunglasses inside?" Holly asked her two companions.

Nash was the first to turn away, grabbing a glass of champagne from a passing server's tray. "I don't think either they or Victor care much. We should go before he gets curious about us."

Quentin plucked two more glasses from the same tray and

handed one to Holly. "Yep, discretion is the better part of valor. Isn't that the way it goes?"

"Did either of you hear what she said? It's like she knows we are here for the scroll regardless of the fact that I told her we weren't earlier today."

"Obviously, she didn't believe you," Nash said.

Holly casually took a sip of her drink. "Should that make me nervous?"

"Oddly enough, I get the impression she likes you, sister. I don't know why she would help you though. Incurring the wrath of the Désorcelers is a death sentence."

"Maybe she's trying to set us up instead," Quentin suggested. With a hand on Holly's lower back, he guided her toward the northernmost part of the building. "But if there is a chance she was trying to help, we should at least check it out."

"You and Nash go. I'll pretend interest in the historical pieces here and alert you if anyone comes your way."

"I'm not comfortable leaving you alone, love."

"With the two of you searching, you're likely to find it faster. I don't think I'll get into trouble with two hundred people mingling about, do you?"

"Okay, but keep a hand on your necklace to let your father listen in."

"I can do that." The worried lines on Quentin's face didn't detract from his masculine beauty. Quite the opposite. Seeing his concern and love made him more attractive to her. She reached up and smoothed the groove between his brows. "I love you, Quentin Buchanan."

He ducked his head and captured her mouth in a sweet, clinging kiss. "And I love you, Holly Anne Thorne. Stay safe."

"That's the plan."

After they'd gone, she chanced a glance over her shoulder to where she'd last seen Victor. He didn't look pleased with Selene. In fact, they appeared deep in a heated discussion.

As if he sensed her regard, he lifted his head to stare in her direction. Her heart rate doubled. Caught, Holly smiled politely and raised her glass before turning away. So much for that plan to stay safe. Quentin was going to murder her for attracting Victor's notice.

She wasn't surprised when Victor spoke from beside her only a short while later.

"I couldn't help but notice you. It isn't every day that an incredibly beautiful woman toasts you."

Holly's hand crept to the necklace at her throat. She wrapped her hand around the stone. "Yes, well, I wanted to ask Selene about donating to her charity but didn't want to interrupt. You happened to catch me glancing that way. It seemed rude to not acknowledge you."

Victor's eyes crinkled with his evil delight. "Of course."

"Get the hell away from him, Holly!"

The smile Holly gave Victor had to scream fake. "If you'll excuse me, I see a friend. I must say hello."

"I'm hurt that you desire to run away, Ms. Thorne."

"You have me at a disadvantage. I'm afraid I don't know who you are."

"I'm an old friend of your father's. You should ask him about me."

"Fuck!"

She jerked at the emphatic swearing on the other side of her telepathic connection. Alastair wasn't given to displays of that nature.

"Should I simply describe you when I see him, since you haven't properly introduced yourself yet?" she asked archly.

The air crackled around them, and Holly glanced about, wondering who might have caused the disturbance in the Force. When her father stepped from behind a column dressed to the nines in a black tuxedo, she didn't bat an eyelash. Why should she be surprised when it was obvious how much he detested Victor?

"Well, Alastair Thorne, as I live and breathe. Come to take your little duckling back to the nest?" Victor taunted.

Alastair put a hand on Holly's shoulder. The arctic smile he gave Victor chilled her to the bone. In a casual tone laced with frost, he said. "Go fuck yourself, Victor. Stay away from my daughter, or I will unleash a hell on you the likes of which you've never seen before."

"I've seen you stripped bare and writhing in pain, Alastair. Your threats seem empty."

The blatant reference to the time when Alastair was held captive in Zhu Lin's dungeon was meant to draw blood. The champagne in Victor's glass began to steam, and to avoid a burn, he quickly set it on a side table.

"Try me. As you can see, I don't have magical shackles binding me this time, Salinger."

The air fairly sizzled between the two men. If hatred had a smell, it would easily overwhelm the room and send people running for the open air outdoors.

"Even *you* wouldn't dare conjure magic here, Thorne. Not in a place protected by the Council."

"As if I've ever given two shits about Council rules."

Victor smiled in triumph. It was as if by saying the words, Alastair had played right into his hands.

A shiver of unease chased down Holly's spine, and she covered the hand on her shoulder. "Let's explore, father. There are a lot of wonderful items to see."

The two adversaries stood locked in a battle of wills. Neither wanted to be the first to give any concession.

Quentin's arrival allowed Holly to breathe a sigh of relief. His arm encircled her from behind as Alastair's dropped to his side.

"Making friends, love?"

While she had felt protected by her father's presence, the solid feel of Quentin's large frame at her back made her relax. "I'm afraid I'm attracting people my father doesn't approve of."

"Well, no offense, Hol, but you do seem to attract the riff-raff."

Victor's dark eyes shot fire at the insult.

"Be careful who you insult, Mr. Buchanan."

"I'm always careful who I insult, Mr. Salinger."

Holly dug her nails into Quentin's hand in warning. The gesture attracted Victor's notice. His smile was heavily laced with contempt.

"You do seem to attract the *riff-raff* as Mr. Buchanan so eloquently stated. If you should ever decide to stop slumming and date a real man, give me a call."

Although not audible, Quentin's low growl reverberated inside her. She tightened her grasp on his arm and leaned back into him.

"Quentin is as far from slumming as it gets, Mr. Salinger. I won't be trading him in anytime soon."

Quentin pulled her closer.

With a keen eye and a slight smirk, Salinger studied them. "No, I can see why you wouldn't when he is easily led about by you. Still, the offer of a real man stands."

Their group waited in silence until Victor was too far away to hear them. Without taking his eyes from Salinger's back, Alastair let loose his fury. "Tell me, boy, why would you ever leave her alone when you knew our worst enemy was in the room?"

"Dad—"

"I entrusted you with her care, and yet you willfully ignored my warning about Victor."

Other than to wrap his other arm around her, Quentin remained motionless and silent.

Holly refused to allow Alastair to take out his anger on him. "You're being completely unfair to Quentin, Dad. You're the one who assigned him the task of finding the scroll. You can't berate him for doing as you requested when I was perfectly safe in a roomful of witnesses."

Alastair turned his disbelieving stare on her. "Safe? What about Victor do you consider safe, Holly Anne?"

"I'm not fool enough to believe he's an angel, but neither did I believe he would attempt to hurt me inside a Council stronghold."

For a long moment, her father said nothing. The change in him was like night and day when it happened. All his anger dissipated, and he cast her a wry smile. "Forgive me. Old wounds and all."

"I think Quentin's the one you should ask for forgiveness."

Alastair's smile widened, and he acknowledged her words by

holding out his hand to Quentin. "Please forgive me, son. I was a bit overcome."

"If we are being honest, my heart stopped when I felt the atmospheric change signaling your arrival. I was certain something terrible had happened to Holly." He sighed heavily. "I'm sorry, sir."

"It's all well and good. Tell me you got what you came for."

"No, sir. I suspect the original item was already swapped for another."

"Explain."

"The item listed as the Cheirotonia Scroll in the display case isn't what we are looking for."

"I told you it would be in the vault, boy. Do you never listen?"

"Dad!"

Alastair grimaced. "Again, my apologies."

"Nothing to forgive, sir. I had hoped a museum worker was careless and put the original on display." Quentin shrugged as if it were no skin off his back. "Nash is still looking for the vault. While you told me it exists on the premises and gave me the spell to unlock it, you never gave me an indication where the damned thing was located."

"Because it is always shifting locations," Alastair answered simply.

"What does that mean?" Holly demanded. "It's never in the same room?"

"Exactly. I had hoped you would be able to obtain the information from the lovely Selene, but..." Alastair tugged at his cuffs and shrugged.

"You underestimated your daughter," Quentin laughed. "Speaking of Selene, she's heading this way."

Holly shifted to welcome the newcomer. "Selene, this is my father—"

"Alastair Thorne," he said smoothly as he held out his hand.

Eyes round with wonder, Selene slipped her hand in his. For once, her blatant sexuality was banked. One had to assume it was the awe of meeting a legend of Alastair's magnitude.

"Mr. Thorne," she breathed.

"Dad, this is Selene Barringer. She's the curator of the museum and head of the Greek branch of the Witches' Council." Holly performed the introductions as if they weren't all well aware of who Selene was.

Raising Selene's hand to his lips, Alastair placed a light kiss on her knuckles. "Charmed."

"I can see where your children get their looks."

A jaunty grin was Alastair's response, and even Holly had to blink in wonder. When had she ever seen this side of her father? Probably never. "Should you two get a room?" Holly snarked.

Selene's breathy laugh caught the attention of those closest to them—Victor included. His scowl sobered her in an instant. "It was a pleasure to meet you, Mr. Thorne. I must go, but may I put you down for a sizable donation for the children's home? This particular gala is to raise funds for a charity near and dear to my heart."

"Not to be callous, but why does a children's home warrant your attention?"

Holly gasped. Leave it to her father to dive right in and get to the truth.

Selene patted Holly's arm and smiled. "I'm not offended." Selene cast a telling glance Victor's way before she confided, "I was orphaned at a formative time in my life. I have a soft spot for others like me."

"I'm sorry, Selene." And Holly truly was. She'd lost her own mother to stasis at a time in her life when she needed her the most.

Selene's earnest, dark eyes locked on Holly. "It's why I intend to help you," she said in a low tone. "Deny it all you want, but I know what you are seeking and why. You have less than one hour before the vault shifts positions. The current location is in the northernmost chamber of the museum. In order to find it, you need a reverse cloaking spell."

She held out a hand to Holly, who took it without pausing to think. The crinkle of a folded square of paper caught her attention.

She didn't dare look down. Instead, she shook Selene's hand and withdrew.

"Thank you, Selene. Should you ever need anything in return, all you need do is ask."

"As I said, you and I would have been great friends. Good luck, Holly."

CHAPTER 19

*A*s one, they watched Selene disappear into the crowd. They continued their pretext of partygoers for another ten minutes to throw off suspicion. Alastair removed a card from his pocket, jotted a note, and asked a waiter to give it to Selene at his first opportunity.

"What did you write down?"

"It was the number for my business manager and a promise for one million dollars for her charity."

Holly stared in disbelief. "Is it crass to ask how much my own father is worth?"

"You can ask, but until my death, you won't find out. Which is to say, don't do anything to hasten my demise, all right?"

"I think you just told me I'm in the will. We're all good." She bit her lip to hold back a laugh. "Besides, I know you never took away my trust fund."

His deep chuckle made her smile in return. "You could have made a withdrawal from your account at any time."

Quentin's head whipped around, and his mouth dropped open. "Trust fund? If she had a trust fund, why the hell was she waitressing at that dive?"

"Because it irritated my father," she quipped. "It gave me great pleasure to see him scowl every time he walked through the doors to the diner or was forced to drink the mud they call coffee."

When Alastair's gaze connected with Quentin and the men laughed, she demanded to know the joke.

Quentin obliged her. "Your dad always magically altered the coffee to a more palatable drink. I was the idiot who always drank the 'mud.'"

"If you ever doubted he loved you, child, that should clear it up."

She bit her lip to hold back the laughter bubbling inside.

"I think we've made a good show of it. You and Quentin find the vault. I'll remain here to keep an eye on Salinger. Go check in with your brother. It's been too long since anyone has heard from him."

Quentin guided her toward the north hall as she whipped out her smartphone and shot off a text to Nash.

His response was instantaneous.

"I think I've found it. Get here."

Holly pulled up the find-my-phone app that allowed her to track Nash's location. They made a right turn down the corridor and entered the first room on the left.

"I thought you'd never get back here," he stated dryly.

"Holly was schmoozing up to Victor. I had to bluster, bark, and piss to mark my territory."

Nash turned his head, but not before Holly saw his amused grin. "There's an intermittent energy pulse coming from this corner. I tried a standard Council spell to unveil the source of the pulse, but it didn't work."

"Try this." Holly handed him the folded paper Selene had provided.

After unfolding it, he shook his head. "This explains why I couldn't do it on my own, there needs to be four of us."

"One sec." Holly gripped the stone at her neck. *"You're needed. Second right past the curator's office, first room on the left."*

"I'll be there momentarily."

"Dad's on his way. What do we need to do to set up in the meantime?"

"Here, conjure these top two items on the list. I'll conjure the rest. Quentin, keep an eye out for trouble. It will follow Alastair."

Holly hiked up her gown above her knees and squatted. Closing her eyes, she held out her hands, palms facing downward, and conjured five large candles. Next, she envisioned a mortar and pestle for the herbs they would use. As she finished, Alastair stepped through the doorway and assisted her to her feet.

"Is this all we need?"

"According to Selene's list, it is," Nash confirmed. "Close the door and let's take our places."

With a simple sweep of his arm, Alastair lifted the candles and set them around the perimeter of the circle. The wicks flickered to life.

"Neat party trick," Quentin muttered as he took his place beside her.

"He knows how to do all the cool stuff," Holly laughed.

"Our time is limited. Join hands and let's be done with this," Alastair ordered.

They all put on their serious faces and clasped hands.

Nash cast the circle and recited the words he'd memorized from the paper.

"Goddess, hear our plea,
assist us in our time of need.
Illuminate for us this item we seek.
Lift the veil, to us the vault reveal."

The wall to Nash's left shimmered and disappeared, revealing the vault door—an imposing ten feet high by eight feet wide.

"I'm glad that worked. It was an embarrassing rhyme," Holly said to no one in particular. "Whoever created that spell should be shot."

Quentin snorted beside her, and her father shot them both a quelling glance.

"I'm just sayin'."

"Time to unlock this beast," Nash declared. "Sperm Donor, do you want to do the honors?"

Alastair shook his head and straightened his collar. "Be my guest. In all likelihood, it will be warded against me anyway. We don't need a spell to backfire at this pivotal moment."

Nash spoke the words to disengage the locks, then stepped forward to swing the door wide.

"I have to say, that was a much better spell," Holly said in an aside to Quentin.

"Yeah, I think there are a few wannabe poets on the Council. Let's go."

"No!" Alastair warned. "Not all of us at once."

"He's right." Nash gestured Quentin forward. "It's a fail-safe. If more than one person sets foot on that floor, a gas is released that will put us all out and seal the vault with us inside. Only a high official of the Council will be able to open the door. And you can only guess how many guards that official would have at their back."

"This might have been something you warned us about before now," Quentin told him sourly. "What if it was only me and Holly here alone?"

"You wouldn't have been able to find the vault, now would you?" Alastair mocked.

Quentin's dark brows clashed together as he glared at her father. From his pocket, he withdrew a manila envelope. He slid out the faux scroll, rolled it, and tied it with a frayed red ribbon he pulled from his pocket.

"Think this will pass muster?"

Holly shrugged. She didn't know what the original artifact looked like, but this one looked authentically ancient. "Looks good to me."

"My understanding is that once I touch the scroll, I may be shot back in time. I don't know if it's instantaneous or not." He shot a meaningful look at Alastair. "Don't wait. If you have to leave me behind for the safety of everyone else, you do that."

Holly grabbed his sleeve. "No!"

"I know better than to ask *you*, love. I'm relying on your father and Nash to get you to safety if things go wrong."

Quentin gathered her close and pressed her ear to his chest. "Hear that, Hol?" She nodded once as she listened to the fast thudding of his heart. "It beats only for you." With one knuckle, he raised her chin as he bent his head. "Only for you." In his kiss, she felt all the things left unsaid.

He pulled away with a wink. "See you on the flip side, my prickly pear."

As goodbyes went, it was romantic as hell. She only hoped this was more of a "see you soon" than a forever type of goodbye.

The second he stepped over the threshold to the vault, the massive door swung shut behind him with a resounding boom.

"That wasn't supposed to happen!" The alarmed look that took the place of Nash's astonishment made Holly's heart stop.

"What do you mean that wasn't supposed to happen?"

"We need to get out of here," Alastair informed them grimly.

"No! No! I'm not leaving Quentin!"

Father and son shared a resolute glance, and Holly knew they didn't intend for her to have a say in the matter. She backed away as Nash charged for her.

"No!"

"*Quiet,*" Alastair hissed. "Listen. Someone's coming, and I promise you, it's not going to be pretty. Take your brother's arm."

"I'm not leaving him."

Alastair strode purposefully forward and touched a finger to her forehead. "*Dormio.*"

Her world went black as her legs collapsed beneath her.

ALASTAIR CAUGHT Holly before she hit the floor. "Take her home, son. I'll clean up this mess."

"Father—"

"Please, do as I say. Get her to safety. I'll be right behind you."

Before he could blink, Nash and Holly were gone. He turned the lock on the door and swiped a hand over the circle, effectively closing it and removing the evidence of their arrival.

He cast one last regretful look at the disappearing vault before he visualized Holly's living room. One by one, his cells heated to burning, but when the warmth receded, he stood in the clearing by Thorne Manor.

"What the devil?"

Alastair spun in a circle and grabbed his head as a wave of dizziness washed over him. When he could get his bearings, he scanned the area around him. How had he come to be here? A sliver of unease chased down his spine. He found it difficult to recall what he was doing in the moments prior to arriving in the glen.

The energy in the clearing shifted, and as he watched, a tall young man with long, dark hair and a self-important swagger started in his direction.

"Hello, Mr. Thorne. I've only got a few minutes. I need you to listen very carefully to what I have to say."

"Who are you?"

"My name is Quentin Buchanan, and as crazy as this sounds, I've come from the future to warn you." When Alastair would have protested or, in all probability, blasted the arrogant pup back from whence he came, the man offered him a piece of paper. "You gave me this to give to you."

Cautiously, as if the note were a snake, Alastair reached for and unfolded it. His neat cursive was penned on the paper in front of him.

"What day is today?" he demanded.

"August twenty-third, two-thousand-eight. The day before I meet your daughter Holly. In order to save her life, I need you to stop that meeting from happening."

CHAPTER 20

Quentin watched the play of emotions cross Alastair's face as he explained the circumstances. His sympathy for Holly's father kicked up a notch as he watched Alastair struggle to wrap his mind around the situation they found themselves in. To have a virtual stranger show up and give you a note—hand-written by yourself—that outlined things to come, had to be confusing as hell and a little bit terrifying. Yet, the other man remained composed as if this type of situation happened every day.

"The long and short of it is that I love your daughter, sir. Enough that, in the future when faced with the necessity of walking away to save her life, I'll do it."

Alastair raised fathomless blue eyes from the paper in his hand to study Quentin. "To clarify, in another timeline, you will meet my daughter tomorrow at school. The two of you will fall in love, but due to a couple of disreputable characters, a misunderstanding occurs. This misunderstanding causes my daughter to marry a man who attempts to murder her in a few years' time. You step in and save her, but then you spend the better part of a decade as a sort of watchdog to protect her from any future harm. Do I have this straight?"

"Pretty much."

"A scroll—what did you call it?"

"The Cheirotonia Scroll."

"Right. This Cheirotonia Scroll allows you—a Traveler Warlock —to travel through time, and you've done this multiple times in the past to abort Holly's death."

"Yes, sir."

"And now, in an attempt to break the cycle, to forestall the stabbing from happening at all, you want me to stop my headstrong daughter from falling in love with you."

Quentin frowned. Did he? Not if there was a better option, but in all the scenarios he'd played through since finding out he needed to return to rescue Holly and rid the earth of Beau Hill, this option seemed the best.

"Son, if you truly love her, why would you ever want to walk away?"

Having Alastair put into words the very question plaguing his soul made Quentin wonder if he wasn't the dumbest fucker on the planet. Swallowing past the lump in his throat, he met the steady gaze of the man in front of him.

"I don't want to walk away. I would lay down my life for Holly. But this vicious cycle needs to stop. Over three hundred times we've played out the coming trauma. If I could give her a happy life, a safer life, by walking away, why wouldn't I?"

With a deep sigh, Alastair meticulously folded the paper in his hand and placed it in his breast pocket. "What is the name of the future husband who stabs her?"

"Beau Hill."

"And the woman who helps him?"

"Michelle Wright."

"To be clear, if these two people never learn Holly is a witch, never conspire against the two of you, then you and Holly will be happy together."

He nodded. "In theory. That would be my fondest wish."

"She loves you? My daughter?"

"She does." A warm smile overtook his face.

"Did you ever betray my daughter in the alternate timeline, boy?"

"No, sir. Never once." Quentin answered honestly. "I'd rather cut out my heart than hurt Holly."

Alastair studied him for a long moment before he nodded once and held out his hand. "I'll make sure your wish is honored, son."

Tears burned Quentin's eyes, and he swallowed hard. "Thank you, Mr. Thorne."

The shadows around them deepened and receded.

A quick check of his surroundings showed the landscape fading.

"I'm out of time. Please remember what I said, and know Holly loves you, sir. She's acting out now, but it's only because she's hurting. She misses her mother and is angry you kept her sisters from her."

"She knows about Rorie's other daughters?"

"And Summer. I can't say any more without drastically altering the timeline. Bring Holly to Athens on—"

The shadows deepened further, and Alastair faded altogether. Quentin's words were lost to the emptiness. He was left to wonder if Holly's father had heard his last request.

If Quentin had to detail the next moments, he'd describe the "warp speed" screen of Star Trek's U.S.S. Enterprise. Lights came at him at such a rate as to be indistinguishable from one another. He was forced to close his eyes against the shifting landscape or risk a seizure.

When the world around him stopped spinning, he was able to get his bearings. The one thing he hadn't expected upon returning was the woman strolling about and touching the ancient magical objects with a reverent stroke of her hand. Although, if he were asked, he would have said he didn't know what to expect. Possibly the entire Council standing by with armed guards?

"Exalted One!" Quentin knelt on one knee to give Athena her due.

"Rise, child."

When she held out her hand, he placed the rolled parchment

within her grasp. Without bothering to look at what she held, she set it alight with a simple touch of her finger.

An emotion akin to panic squeezed Quentin's lungs, and he surged forward. "No! I need that!"

"And you shall have it with you always. Open your shirt."

Cautiously, he unknotted his tie and stuffed it in his pocket. Next, he slowly unbuttoned his shirt to expose his chest.

Her curious aqua eyes ran the length of his torso. "You are a fine specimen, Quentin. A true child of the Gods."

"What does that mean?"

She smiled as she moved toward him. "You are a descendent of my father, Zeus. Did you not know?"

"I had no idea. My family's lineage was lost over time."

Athena frowned and glanced to her left. A leather-bound book of spells rested on a wooden stand. "Lost, you say?"

"That's the story."

"It must be why you never understood the true extent of your abilities."

"I can do more than blast air, teleport, and time travel?" he asked with a laugh.

"Yes, much more. We will get into that later. First, let us finish this." Without warning, she pressed the ball of ash to the place over his heart.

The searing agony made him gasp and want to retch. The smell of burning flesh only added to his nausea. *"What the fuck?"*

Her brows climbed up toward her hairline, but she didn't scold him for his language. Instead, she waved her hand over the branded skin. The redness disappeared and, with it, any residual pain. He studied the mark on his left pec.

"An owl?"

"You need to make it a priority to study your Greek ancestors, child." The chiding quality was heavy in her tone. "The owl is a symbol of wisdom and courage. *My* symbol. It will allow you to take flight whenever you need to, from now to the end of your life cycle. This is my gift to you." She buttoned his shirt and straightened his jacket. "You need only think about where you wish to go, and you will be able to achieve it."

"Thank you, Exalted One. You are too generous."

"You are deserving. If you were not, you would receive no help from the Gods."

"Gods plural?"

"Who do you think originally sent me?"

"I'm going out on a limb here and saying Zeus?"

She laughed. "I have two more gifts for you. But we must hurry now. Time will correct itself in mere seconds."

"I thought it had when I returned?"

She literally rolled her eyes, causing Quentin to laugh. Who knew goddesses were so human in nature?

"I can tell I have a lot to learn."

"Yes, child, you do. This should help you." She stepped over to the book she had glanced at earlier. "Your family's grimoire." She thumbed through the pages until she came to a particular spot. She held out both hands and conjured two additional objects. One, a simple bookmark which she slipped between the pages before closing the book again. The other was a small crystal globe, pink in color and about three inches in diameter. It resembled nothing more than a giant marble. The center constantly shifted and swirled, mesmerizing him.

"I've marked the spell you will need for future travel." Her words snapped him out of his daze. She beckoned him to join her. "You will take the book and this object—the Heart of Artemis—with you when you leave here. I've charmed them both, and none will see you leave."

"What's the deal with the Heart of Artemis? Is it a type of quest I need to accomplish for you?"

She smiled and patted his cheek. "You are delightful." She handed him the object, and as it touched his hand, it flared to life with a pulsing glow. "Careful. This was never meant for your use."

"I don't understand."

"It is a bride's gift for your young woman."

"The only woman I'll ever marry is Holly Thorne, and she was lost to me today."

Athena cast him a mysterious look. "Was she?"

His confusion grew. Had he not changed the timeline? Why were his memories of Holly so crisp? Shouldn't they have faded as history changed? He asked as much of Athena. Her answer surprised him.

"Alastair Thorne didn't alter your meeting with Holly Thorne as you requested."

Quentin closed his eyes and swayed. This time he was sure he was going to heave up his guts. Without him to stop Beau that night, Holly would have been killed.

"He didn't alter your meeting, but he did remove the threat."

His eyes snapped open, and he stared in shocked wonder.

"It's time for you to remember the new timeline, Quentin Buchanan." In a stunningly swift move, she tapped his temple.

Memories, new and old, merged in his head. Mostly, they were images of him and Holly as they were and as they continued on in their relationship without interference from Beau or Michelle. The clearest picture of all was that of Holly, belly rounded with his child. Their love was deeply entrenched.

"Holly's pregnant?" he asked in disbelief.

"She is. She's waiting for you in the gardens outside. You must hurry."

"I want so badly to hug you right now," he told her.

Athena nodded toward the door. "You still have trials ahead, but I have no doubt you will prevail. Go."

Quentin scooped up the book and the Heart of Artemis, and before he could second guess his boldness, he kissed her cheek. Her beatific smile stole his breath away.

"Rascal."

"Thank you for everything."

"Come back to my city and visit, dear boy."

"You know it."

The mammoth vault door swung wide as he approached. To his astonishment, no one was on the other side.

"The Gods still wield power, and the Witches' Council listens." Athena spoke from behind him.

"They wouldn't dare not," he agreed with a grin.

They shared an understanding glance. He imagined it would be a long while before—or if—he ever saw her again. Because he couldn't not say it, he spoke the words in his heart. "You've given me my life back. It would have been a cold and dreary existence without Holly. I owe you everything."

She cleared her throat and shooed him out of the vault. "Begone. I have other mortals' messes to clean up."

Quentin tucked the globe into the interior pocket of his tuxedo jacket, gripped the grimoire tightly, and dashed for the garden by the café. Although he received curious looks from the partygoers, no one stopped him or questioned his haste. As he rounded the side of the building, his heart dropped to his big toe.

Victor Salinger and his goons surrounded Holly, Nash, and Alastair. Selene was going toe-to-toe with him. With little to no expression on his face, Victor withdrew a pistol with a silencer attached and promptly shot her point blank.

Holly dropped her brother's hand and rushed to the fallen Selene.

Even from this distance, Quentin heard her rage.

"You motherfucker! She was your *sister!* What kind of cold-ass bastard shoots his own sister?"

Instinctively, he started to close his fist, but then an idea took hold. If Holly was allowed free rein of her temper, would birds swoop down and pluck out Victor's cold, beady eyes? When no birds appeared, Quentin realized the problem, Holly was touching another Thorne—*the one in her womb.*

Victor turned the gun on her. "She betrayed me to help you. She knew the consequences of her actions."

Across the distance, Alastair met Quentin's panicked gaze but then shifted his attention to a point beyond his left shoulder. Before Quentin could turn, Athena spoke. "I had hoped you would arrive before the drama. Come. Let us clear up this little problem, shall we?"

"You do know you'd make the perfect mate for Alastair Thorne, don't you? Both of you cool as cucumbers and droll as fuck," Quentin muttered, his heart pounding out of his chest.

Her laughter drew the attention of the group.

Snapping to attention, Victor's security detail trained their weapons on Quentin and Athena. Her laughter turned deeper, more throaty and wicked. "Foolish mortals," she admonished as she glided forward. "You come to my city, create wars with one another, and fail to pay homage to the Gods and Goddesses who rule here."

Alastair and Nash each hastily took a knee next to Holly. The three Thornes bowed their heads in respect. Victor and his crew didn't realize their mistake until it was too late.

Athena lifted her arms skyward, summoning a maelstrom of weather. Lightning flashed, bringing an immediate pop of thunder. Lashing rain came from every direction.

Quentin ran to Holly. He knelt in front of her with his back to Victor. He tucked her into his chest to protect her from the threat of bullets and the raging storm.

Quentin doubted Athena would let Victor get a shot off, but he wasn't taking any chances. Whatever it took, he would protect Holly and his unborn child.

"I thought you'd never get here," she whispered. "What took so long?"

He flashed her a roguish grin. "I was making time with Athena in the vault."

Holly's eyes darted toward the goddess. "Yeah, well, I'll forgive you this one time. Thanks for bringing a goddess as backup."

"Put your guns down, you fools!" Victor shouted over the storm at his minions even as he knelt and bowed his head. "Goddess, please, forgive me."

"You dare too much, Victor Salinger. Your ancestors should have taught you manners and to pay homage to the old ones. Instead you would take life without permission."

As Victor's face lost color and as he hemmed and hawed his excuses to Athena, Holly pulled Quentin away and nodded toward

Selene's unconscious figure. "What can we do to help her? I think she's bleeding out."

Because he knew touching Selene was out of the question due to the poison now coursing through her veins, Quentin sought help from Athena's corner. "Exalted One. She needs assistance."

"I'm sorry, child, but it is her time. She will not suffer."

As the protest formed on Holly's lips, Quentin leaned in and kissed it away. "Stay silent, love. Athena will not be swayed."

"But Quentin—"

"Holly, please don't argue."

When her large, trusting eyes turned up to him, Quentin's heart stuttered in his chest. In this reality, Holly always maintained faith in him, but he still held the memories of their previous timeline. This unfailing belief made Quentin fall in love with her all over again.

"Are you okay?" She cupped his cheek in her palm.

His gaze dropped to her protruding belly. "Yeah, I guess I am, but I want to get you to safety."

The storm died out, and his words could be heard by all.

"You may take your woman home, Quentin Buchanan. Victor and his crew will bother you no more. He now knows you are favored by my father. Should you or your family be hurt, the tortures heaped upon him will be plenty."

"Music to my ears."

Hatred flared to life in Victor's dark, dead eyes. The promise there was clear; if he should ever get the chance to hurt them, he'd take it and damn the consequences.

Quentin strode to where Victor stood silently fuming. "Not only will the tortures of the Gods be heaped upon you, Salinger. I will flay the skin from your bones if you ever look sideways at my wife or future children. Nod your understanding." A slight twitch of Victor's head was all the acknowledgment Quentin received, but it was enough. Never taking his eyes from his enemy, Quentin addressed Athena. "Goddess, with your leave, I will take my wife and her family from Athens."

"Holly Buchanan, step forward."

Holly carefully picked her way to Athena.

Athena nodded to her protruding belly. "May I?" When his wife nodded her agreement, the goddess laid her hands atop the mound. "Your child will possess untold power and will one day be a great leader. She will know suffering, but she will prevail to find the love of a lifetime. This is my blessing for you."

A single tear escaped down Holly's cheek as she smiled her joy. "Thank you, Exalted One. You are all that is gracious and kind."

"Go in peace, children."

CHAPTER 21

"*J* was hoping when Athena called me to her, that she was going to let me kick Victor in the 'nads, or at the very least punch, him in the voice box," Holly grumbled later that evening as they prepared for bed. "Poor Selene. She didn't deserve what she got."

Quentin drew her down on the mattress between his legs to rub the stress from her shoulders and back. "How did you know she was Victor's sister?"

"He said as much before you came out of the museum. When she said she was no longer going to do his bidding, he told her that he should have made sure she drowned in the well on their family estate. Poor Selene turned white." Holly took a shuddering breath. "That's when he shot her."

"I'm sorry you had to witness that, love." Quentin wrapped his arms around her from behind and buried his nose in her neck.

"I thought I was next," she whispered.

"I would have gone back and saved you. I don't care how many times it took." His fervent promise had her attempting to twist and face him. She finally gave up the fight with her bulging belly and stood.

"What happened to the scroll, Quentin?"

"What do you remember of our trip, Hol?"

"I don't understand. You were there for the whole thing, except for your time in the vault."

"No. I think I changed history tonight. That's why I'm asking."

"What? How? That makes no sense."

"Humor me, love. Tell me what you remember about the trip."

"We teleported in together yesterday afternoon. We visited the local touristy sites—until my feet started to throb—then we went back to our hotel suite." She cocked her head to study him.

He gave her a warm smile. In the new timeline, they had ordered room service and spent the afternoon making leisurely love. "Go on."

Her blush assured him that was how she remembered the events too. "We had dinner and then got busy. When I woke from my nap, you were gone. As it got later, I grew concerned and contacted my father through the necklace he gave me. He and Nash arrived to look for you." As he watched, she swallowed hard. "We were all worried when you didn't return. When morning rolled around, you showed up and told me you spent the evening talking to Athena at her temple."

"What next?"

"We all went out to breakfast to plan the heist of the scroll. I may have lost my temper a bit and stormed out."

"A bit?"

"Okay, a lot. Nash didn't want me to be a part of the mission because of my condition." She pulled a face. "I caught a cab and went to the museum where I met Selene. We had tea. Oddly enough, I felt like we bonded in a weird way. We must have because she betrayed Victor in an attempt to help us escape tonight."

"So at some point, you came back from tea with Selene, we all went to the gala, and when I entered the vault, you—along with your father and brother—escaped the Councils' detection with the help of Selene. That's when Victor cornered you outside."

"Exactly." She wove her fingers into his hair and tilted his head back. "I thought my heart would stop when that damned vault door slammed shut. When Nash said that wasn't supposed to happen, I almost died."

"I'm sorry, love. I was never in any danger."

She closed her eyes, and he could practically feel her relief. This connection of theirs, while solid, was still new to him. He wasn't used to being in perfect accord with Holly.

He glanced down at the wedding ring on his left hand.

His wife.

The memories of their wedding day were simply that—memories, and it made him sad to know he'd missed the ceremony. He wanted to experience the joy of exchanging their vows. Of removing her dress, inch by inch, off her silky, shimmering skin and laying her down on a bed covered in rose petals from Spring's garden. Of making love to her until she incoherently screamed his name in her ecstasy.

"Quentin, what's wrong?"

He lifted his head to meet her concerned gaze. "It's hard to explain."

"Because you changed history? How?"

"I don't know if by telling you the past, I'm might break a cosmic rule."

"Was it so very different from now?"

"Yes." He closed his eyes against the pain of the past. "Yes, Hol, it was. I thought you were lost to me forever."

The light, soothing touch of her fingertips as she stroked the planes of his face caused him to open his eyes to her and the truth of their love.

"We'd have always found our way back to one another, my darling man. I'm sure of it."

The sting of tears burned behind his lids and his nasal passages as he struggled to hold the emotion at bay. "Goddess, I love you, Holly. More than you can ever possibly know."

"I love you, Quentin, to the very depths of my soul. I can't imagine a life without you in it." Holly leaned in and lowered her forehead to his. "I'm glad you fixed our timeline to allow us to have all this."

He opened his mouth to respond when she jerked in his arms. "Hol?"

"Our girl is raising a fuss!" She grabbed his hand and placed it on her abdomen. "I guess you were right to paint the nursery pink."

"Pink?"

"You said you had a feeling we were having a girl."

Quentin shook his head in wonder. The memories formed in his mind as if she conjured them with her words. This new reality was going to take some getting used to. He could feel the heel of their daughter's foot as she kicked the wall of Holly's uterus. All he could do was stare in shocked awe. "She's a little badass."

"She totally is," Holly agreed on a laugh. "What are you doing?" she asked on a husky breath when he lifted the edge of her top over her head and tossed it aside.

"I want to see you. All of you." He stripped her bare and trailed his fingers over her curves. "You're beautiful, love."

She snorted her disbelief. "And you're blind."

"No, Hol, you are the most incredible woman I've ever seen." He drew her closer and pressed his lips to her baby mound. "I think it's time to settle on a name."

"What about Francesca?"

Quentin tried it out. "Francesca Anne Buchanan, you get your butt back here this instant!" He nodded. "It works."

"You predict you'll be yelling at her often?"

"I predict, if she is anything like her mother, she'll have me wrapped around her little finger." He grinned and drew her down to straddle his lap. "I was trying the full name out for you since you'll be the disciplinarian."

Holly's throaty laugh curled around his dick and squeezed. "Now, it's time for our little one to go to sleep. Mommy and Daddy need fun time." She smoothed a hand over her belly, then snapped her fingers to dispose of his clothes. "That's better."

"We won't be able to do this much longer," Quentin grunted as she shoved him backward on the bed and sank onto his erection.

"Bite your tongue." She placed his hands on her breasts with a suggestive half-smile. "I say we do this up until the second I go into labor. You with me?"

"Fuck. Yes!"

He cupped her engorged breasts and prayed they would never lose their fullness. When she threw back her head and moaned, Quentin shifted his hips and thrust up in a long, smooth stroke.

"Again," she panted.

They fell into a faster rhythm. When he thought he couldn't hold on another second, Holly shattered in his arms and screamed his name. His own orgasm was put on hold to allow him to stare up into her beautiful flushed face. His heart was as full as it had ever been when she opened her eyes and smiled down at him.

"You going to finish anytime today, stud?" she teased.

"Now you've asked for it."

"And I'm hoping you'll give it to me."

HOLLY WAS DISTURBED out of her sleep by a knock at the bedroom door.

"Holly? Quentin?"

"Summer?"

The door creaked open.

"Hey. What's going on?"

"It's Mom. She's failing. Dad called and said we need to perform the ritual now or we could lose her."

The shock of her sister's words sent her reeling. "Tonight?"

"I know it's a lot to ask after the day you've had…"

"Don't be ridiculous. Of course, I'll help." She turned to gaze up at Quentin who had wordlessly sat up beside her.

"I heard." He looked to Summer. "Head to your dad's. We'll be right behind you."

After Summer left, Holly sat in stunned silence.

"Are you okay, love?"

"I never thought this day would arrive." She bit her lip to hold back the outpouring of words she wanted to say. Anything she told him would be redundant at this point, but it didn't make her nerves any less raw or leave her feeling any less battered. "I don't know how we are going to save her without the scroll."

"I think I do."

Her head snapped around, and she gaped at his smiling face.

"Athena gave me a bride's gift for you. In all the craziness, I forgot to pass it along. She must have foreseen you would need it."

"What is it? A gift to help my mom?"

"I believe it is. It's called the Heart of Artemis."

"I've never heard of it."

"No, but I'll lay odds Nash or your father have."

"I need to get a quick shower. Will you find out what Nash knows?"

"I can do that." He leaned in to drop a light, lingering kiss on her lips. "Stay strong, love. We'll help your mom."

"Thank you." She felt like a live wire—all full of hope and fear, mixed with a ton of trepidation. "I'll meet you at my dad's."

Holly rubbed her lower back and waddled to the bathroom. For a long second, she stared longingly at the jetted garden tub before she stepped into her shower and adjusted the spray settings. A long, relaxing soak would be great, but she'd settle for the next best thing. There was nothing like the overhead waterfall and additional two shower heads to complete the experience. Summer had known what she was doing when she conjured this house last year after coming to town to start her veterinary clinic and animal sanctuary. The spa-like *en suite* bathroom she'd created for Holly's home was to die for.

She lathered herself from head to toe and concentrated on clearing her mind for the upcoming spell. It was important to cleanse all the negative energy to promote better magic. She strongly suspected they were all going to need every added boost they could get. The shower helped to restore and center her, but she still needed one more step.

Adding a few drops each of lavender and rosemary oils into a diffuser, Holly then lowered herself into an armchair with all the grace of a lumbering rhino. She only allowed herself five minutes to meditate because she knew the others would be waiting on her to help revive Aurora. It was scary business. Do or die—literally for her mother.

The underlying concern was whether her mother would wake normal or as a shell of her former self. When her sister Autumn woke from her stasis after having only been in a coma-like state for a few days, she'd been different from her former self. It had taken weeks and a magical boost from Alastair for her to return to a new standard of normal. She'd confessed there was still a small part of her that remained affected after all these months. What did that herald for their poor mother, who had been in stasis for twenty years?

A ripple in the energy of the surrounding air alerted her to another presence. Holly opened her eyes when a knock sounded on her door.

"Come in."

The door swung open, revealing her father. He looked as haggard as she'd ever seen him.

She struggled to rise, but before she could, he was there with an assist. She took his proffered hand and rose to stand in front of him. "Thanks. It's getting a little more awkward to get around these days."

"Are you almost ready, child?"

"I am. I was finishing up." She shrugged. "I wanted to be as clear as possible for the ceremony."

"That's good." He seemed distracted, and the grooves on either side of his mouth were deepened with his worry.

"Are you going to be okay if this doesn't work," she asked softly.

"I don't know. It's highly doubtful."

The confession propelled her into his arms. Her heart ached for him. If the situations had been reversed, she'd probably be the same way. "It's going to be okay, Dad. I promise, regardless of which way this goes, you always have us."

His embrace tightened a millisecond before he released her. "Thank you, darling girl. We should go."

They joined hands, and Holly could feel her cells ramp up twice as fast as he teleported them to the hallway outside of Aurora's room. The others were gathered inside the open doorway of the bedroom.

"Are we doing this here or in the clearing by Thorne Manor?" Spring asked. "The last time, we needed the magic of the stones to revive Autumn."

"Actually, this place is built on another sacred site," Alastair informed them as he stepped forward to scoop up Aurora.

The loving way he cradled her to his chest brought tears to Holly's eyes. As always, Quentin was attuned to her emotions and wrapped her in a warm hug.

"What did you find out about the Heart of Artemis? Did Nash have any ideas?"

"He's searching his library now. He said he'll join us in a few minutes once he discovers what we need."

Together, Holly and Quentin walked hand in hand, following the procession down a long hallway to a set of French doors that opened out onto a quaint garden. Holly had never visited this lovely refuge with its breathtaking view and trickling waterfall. It was a hidden paradise.

"This is freaking amazing!" Autumn said what they were all feeling.

"I created it for your mother. She'll want a place to read when she recovers."

"Jesus, you are really a romantic sonofabitch, aren't you?" Autumn's husband muttered.

"Keaton!"

His cheeks took on a light pink tinge at his wife's scolding. "Sorry."

Alastair surprised them all when he snorted. "It's quite all right. I'm used to the boy being unable to hold his tongue."

"Where's Summer? I thought she arrived before we did," Holly asked. Her sister should have arrived a good twenty minutes ago.

"She's helping Nash search his archive for information on the object Athena gifted you," Alastair informed her. "She should be here momentarily."

They continued on their way in silence. Out through the wrought-iron gate, they traveled single file down a stone path until it became dirt. Still they journeyed to a clearing the length of a football field from the main house.

By the time they arrived, Holly's back was aching like a bitch. The pain was rivaled only by her swollen feet. "What's next?"

"We wait for your brother and sister," her father informed her. The expression on his face was as grim as it got, and Holly wondered if he doubted they had a snowball's chance in hell of succeeding.

CHAPTER 22

*T*hey didn't have long to wait. Summer and Nash broke through the trees within minutes of their group's arrival. Summer was flushed, and her eyes sparkled with excitement.

"That was one hell of a gift Athena gave you, sister!"

Holly was about to ask what they'd found, when Coop spoke up. "You didn't sneeze."

All eyes turned to Summer. She looked confused and glanced around. "Is it the magic of this place?"

Holly squealed when as she realized the significance of the suspended curse. "You're pregnant!"

"What?" Both Summer and Coop parroted in unison. They looked like Holly had whipped out a bat and pulled a Morty on them.

"The only reason you wouldn't sneeze is if you are touching another Thorne, sister."

Summer's hand flew to her flat abdomen as she turned her blue eyes, wide with wonder, on Coop. "We're going to have a baby?"

He laughed and gathered her close. "It would appear so, but I honestly don't know how you wouldn't have figured that out on your own by now."

"Well, you didn't figure it out either!" she retorted.

"It's not my body, sweetheart." He leaned in and whispered in her ear, making the color flare hot in her cheeks.

"Shut it!"

"As much as I love a good Hallmark moment, we should really get this show on the road, sister." Autumn softened her words by running a hand down their sister's long, blonde hair. "Congratulations. Now, tell us. What did you find out?"

"The Cheirotonia Scroll was never going to work for this ritual," Nash informed them. "It was only ever meant for one man's use." He nodded at Quentin. "That would be you. I believe it was why Athena offered up the globe. But, as a Traveler, the Heart of Artemis is the one tool you cannot use. If you do, you take the risk of getting locked in an inter-dimensional time warp. That object is that strong."

"Lovely," Quentin muttered.

Nash dug into his messenger bag and pulled out the globe in question. "I'm assuming Athena gave it to you with a warning?"

"She did." Quentin looked to Alastair. "I'm betting this means I need to sit this one out. We can't take the risk of my magic counteracting that of the other artifacts."

"I think that's wise, son." Alastair gently laid Aurora on the stone altar in the center of the clearing. As he gazed down at her, he asked, "What else did you find about the Heart of Artemis?"

"It's a type of conduit. It's what's going to connect you to the Otherworld and allow Aurora to pass through to this plane. It works in conjunction with the other three artifacts you've collected." Nash approached Aurora and set the globe at the crown of her head. "The problem is that you need seven witches who are blood-related to her, Alastair."

As Holly watched, the life seemed to drain from her father. He'd instantly done the math and realized there were only five direct blood relatives present. "It's over then. There is no way to find her brother in time, and trying to sway any of her living aunts to assist us is pointless. Those old battle-axes are more likely to bring the whole Witches' Council down on our heads rather than help us."

Alastair perched on the edge of the stone and smoothed Aurora's hair on either side of her face. He didn't bother to hide his devastation. "My apologies, my love. I truly thought we could pull this off."

"We have more than seven," Holly said. All eyes turned to where she stood with her hands cradling her unborn babe. "By my count, we have eleven."

"I don't understand," Keaton said. "What the hell are you talking about?"

"Four of the five of us are pregnant. Winnie is sporting triplets in that massive belly of hers," Holly clarified with a grin. "That makes eleven. I should think that is more than enough power between us all. My little muffin is a direct descendant of Zeus."

With a happy laugh, her sisters enfolded her in a group hug. Spring was the first to pull away. She held out her hand to Nash. "Let me look at the spell." When he handed her the sheet of paper, she read through it and nodded at whatever conclusion she'd come to before handing it to her fiancé, Knox. "What do you think?"

"I think your sister is almost as brilliant as you."

"Hey!" Holly laughingly scolded. "Not cool." But they all knew Spring had an IQ off the charts, and she wasn't in the least offended by coming in second to her sister.

Holly turned her attention to her father. "What do you say, Dad? Want to give it a try?"

The line between his brows deepened as he continued to stare down at Aurora. Reaching an internal decision, he glanced up at Nash. "Will it risk the babies?"

"I don't believe so. We can have GiGi on call in the event anything goes wrong."

"Is there a real chance of that?" Winnie's fiancé, Zane, who had remained silent throughout the whole discussion, asked. "I won't risk my children."

"Nor would I," Alastair agreed. "If there is the slightest chance even one of the babies might be harmed, we will abort this plan."

"I don't think Athena would have given Holly the Heart of Artemis if she didn't expect her to use it," Quentin reasoned. "She knew Holly was heavily pregnant when she handed it to me. If everyday magic doesn't hurt the babies, then I can't imagine this would either. A spell is a spell."

Autumn stepped forward. "I agree."

"I'm willing to risk it," Winnie said as she placed a soothing hand on Zane's chest. "She's my mother, Zane."

All four pregnant sisters joined hands, their decision made.

Spring stepped to the others and linked her fingers with Holly's. "The babies' magical powers can only amplify the spell."

When Holly met Alastair's grateful gaze, a sheen of tears shimmered and caused his eyes to brighten in color. She caught her breath. The color of her father's irises hadn't been that light since she was a child, before tragedy had ripped her family apart.

"We're with you, Dad. We can do this. We're Thorne witches, aren't we? It's my understanding that there's no one on this planet as badass as a Thorne."

"Word!" voiced Autumn in agreement. "We've got this, Uncle. And before you get all worried that we don't understand the consequences, we can all assure you, we do." She looked to her sisters for confirmation before she spoke. "We're willing to take the risk. But I'm betting that if Spring believes it's okay, then it is." She shot a warm, confident smile at their youngest sister. "I have faith in her."

Nash stepped forward. "Let's get this show on the road."

"Thank you," Alastair said. The gruffness in his voice spoke of how grateful he was for their assistance.

As Alastair looked out over the next generation of Thorne witches, he felt hope for the first time in a long time. These five women, in addition to his son, were smart, free thinkers who were all courageous to a fault and willing to take on the world if need be. They stood ready to assist him in waking Rorie, at great risk to themselves.

His gaze shifted to their significant others. Three of the four Carlyle men looked uncertain, which was perfectly natural when their unborn children were on the line. But it was Knox Carlyle and

Quentin Buchanan to whom Alastair turned. These men were gifted. Not only in brains, but in powers handed down from the gods and goddesses who watched over them. These men were two of the most powerful people on the planet, yet their easy-going temperaments kept them in check. The Powers That Be had chosen wisely with Knox and Quentin.

Alastair addressed all the men. "I'd feel most comfortable if you all would spread out around the perimeter of the clearing to protect our family. This spell is going to take the bulk of the women's power and will leave them vulnerable during the process." He shrugged. "I don't expect trouble because not many know of this particular location, but I don't want to take any chances. Knox, I'd like you to take the spot at the North end, there." He pointed toward true North. "Quentin, you can guard the South spot on the path where we came in. The rest of you spread out between the two of them. Please keep your eye on the tree line." He removed his tanzanite ring and handed it to Nash. "My overseer has cameras and sensors all over this area to detect movement. Wear this. It will give you a psychic connection to him should he need to warn us of any impending attack."

"Isn't this all overkill? How could anyone know we intend to do this here and now?"

"I'm not taking any chances, son. Our family has too many enemies. Victor Salinger was put in his place and humiliated by Athena only today. Or at least that's how he would see it."

"I understand." Nash slipped on the ring and went to Spring to collect the amulet known as Thor's hammer. "I believe you have the last remaining piece, cousin."

"I was told never to take it off by Nephthys."

He stared at her for a long moment. "Fair enough. We'll do this with it in place. In that case, you'll need to stand on the left side of the altar and be ready to place your hand over your mother's heart, like you did when you brought Knox back to life. I have the herbs we'll need." To the others, he said, "We are going to make a tighter circle because it is only you five. Alastair will stand within the circle of stones, but outside of your circle. One of you will need to memorize this spell." He held out the paper, and Summer stepped forward to take it. "Each of you will call on your elemental magic and the God or Goddess of the object you possess as Summer recites the spell. Autumn, the Chintamani Stone. Spring, Thor's Hammer. Winnie, the Uterine Amulet. Holly, the Heart of Artemis. When you are able to harness the power, direct it to Alastair. He will open the portal. Any questions?"

Winnie raised her hand as if she were in the schoolroom addressing her teacher. "We all represent the four elements..." She gestured to herself, Autumn, Spring, and Holly. "...but how does Summer figure into this? Will a second water elemental offset the balance?" She cast an apologetic glance at Summer. "I don't mean to exclude you in the least."

"I'm not offended, sister. I understand your reasoning."

Nash placed a hand on Summer's shoulder and squeezed. "Actually, Summer has the ability to stop time. That will come in handy for the transfer of Aurora's spirit from one plane to the next when Alastair recites his part of the spell."

Watching Nash, Alastair felt a deep paternal pride. Whether Nash wanted to admit it or not, he was a chip off the old block. Had things worked out differently in Alastair's life, he might have been the one in charge of the North American Witches' Council. But he'd had a falling out with them long ago when they freely sacrificed him to Zhu Lin in order to save their own worthless hides. Though it had been decades past, Alastair wasn't likely to forgive or forget.

The world viewed him as a rebel and a black sheep. He was perfectly content to let that impression stand. He knew the truth, as did those in the high seats of the Council. One day, he'd settle the score. For now, Rorie was his priority. The moment she was out of the woods, he'd take care of Victor Salinger.

"If you all are comfortable with Nash's explanation, let us begin," he said. "This will begin like the spell for—"

The air molecules around them shifted, and a rift opened on the far side of the clearing.

"Incoming. Be prepared!"

They all breathed a collective sigh of relief when his brother, Preston, along with GiGi and Ryker stepped through the rip.

"You are always hosting these little parties without me, brother," GiGi scolded with a pretend pout. "I'm getting a complex."

"I wasn't the one who sent out the invitations. That would be your nephew, Nash."

"I'm sorry, Aunt GiGi. If it's any consolation, I fully intended to call you."

"Come, dear boy. Give me a kiss, and all is forgiven." She pointed to her alabaster cheek.

Nash laughed and dutifully kissed her.

"Now, how can I help?"

Alastair met his brother's worried amber gaze across the distance. "Thank you for coming, Pres."

They appeared as dissimilar as two siblings could be. Preston's was a stockier frame, and his dark auburn hair always seemed to be permanently mussed, whereas Alastair was blond without a hair out of place. Preston's look lent to his absent-minded-professor air. Only when one looked past the surface did they recognize their mistake. Preston Thorne was wickedly intelligent and tended to be just as ruthless and unforgiving as Alastair.

"I wouldn't miss it, Al." In this, his younger sibling was kinder and more giving. Alastair envied the beautiful side of Preston's personality. A part, he long doubted he possessed himself. While his little brother was quick to temper, mostly he had an innate sense of fairness. Along the way, he'd thrown away his hurt and anger over Aurora returning to Alastair.

He knew he couldn't be as accepting if their situation were reversed. Hell, he hadn't been. When he'd returned home from the witches' war to find Rorie had married Preston, Alastair lost what was left of his mind. He didn't sleep, didn't eat. The rampage he'd gone on was epic. When Rorie sought him out to explain, Alastair was finally able to rein in his savagery. The magical world as a whole had breathed a sigh of relief.

Over the last eighteen years, he wasn't any less angry at his loss.

No, he just learned to hide it better. He sighed heavily and brought his thoughts back to the matter at hand.

"We were getting ready to cast. The children have it covered inside the circle, and I had planned to act as a conduit to anchor Rorie to this plane."

"And if you can't convince her to step through?"

"I'll chase her to the Otherworld and bring her home if I have to."

Preston dropped his gaze, but not before Alastair saw the flash of pity. It came to him then that his siblings didn't really believe he could revive his beloved. They all thought he'd been on a fool's errand this entire time.

"Preston, may I speak with you in private?"

Surprise lit his brother's countenance, but Preston quickly joined him at the edge of the clearing out of earshot of the others.

"I need you to make me a promise."

"No!" Preston shook his head. "Not again. Not this time."

"Please, hear me out, brother."

The mutinous expression on his little brother's face said he had no intention of listening.

Alastair grabbed his arm when he would've stormed away. "Please. In all our lives, I've only asked you for one thing; to take care of Summer. And in that, you had your own selfish reasons. Now I need another favor."

"What? What is this damned favor, Al?" Preston snapped as he spun back around. "Don't tell me; let me guess. If things go wrong, you want me to end you. Do I have that right? You want to join Aurora on the other side."

"I do."

"Goddammit, Alastair!" With his hands laced behind his head, Preston paced back and forth. Every five or six seconds, he would shake his head like an angry bear and glare at Alastair.

"How can you ask this of me?" he finally asked. *"How?"* Preston closed his eyes and swallowed. "You're my big brother. I love you. GiGi loves you, as do all the children—your son included, although he would go to his grave denying it. How can you be willing to throw it all away for a woman who is already gone?"

"I'm tired, Preston. Bone weary to my very soul tired. Reviving Rorie is what I have lived for these past years." Alastair studied the forest beyond the clearing. "If I'm forced to admit it, I'm lonely, too. Seventy-five years is a good, long life, brother."

He faced Preston. The ravaged expression on his face tore at Alastair's heart.

"What say you?"

"I can't..." Preston cleared his throat. "...I can't stop you if you want to go. I can only ask you not to. I can only tell you our families will be exceedingly sad if you aren't there for the births of their children. Who will slip the little ones their favorite candy when their parents tell them no?"

Alastair chuckled at the knowing look in his brother's eye. "You knew that was me, huh?"

"I think the sticky faces gave it away. Not to mention Winnie never quite saw the point of lying to her mother and father. Also, Ryker was highly offended when I accused him of ruining their dinner."

Alastair shot Ryker the stink-eye from where they stood. "Don't let that lying S.O.B. tell you he didn't sneak them treats from time to time. I wasn't the only one who spoiled your children."

"No, but you did spoil them a little more frequently than I would've liked."

He gave his younger brother a shrug and a half-hearted smile. "What can I say, Pres? You make adorable children."

Preston snorted, then turned serious. "Whatever you decide, I will honor. I only ask that you reconsider what you mean to this family, big brother."

"I can offer you that much."

His brother started to step away but paused a few feet from him. "Al? Have you ever worried about the consequences of bringing Rorie back? Of what she will be like after this much time? How much of her soul will be lost?"

"I have."

"And you still want to do this, even knowing she could be an entirely different person?"

"I do."

With a heartfelt sigh, Preston joined the others.

Alastair took one deep, calming breath and followed suit.

CHAPTER 23

*F*or the initial raising of the standing stones, all the
Thornes participated except Nash and Summer.

For Holly, this was her first experience with such a powerful
ceremony. To feel the ground rumble and witness the wide pillars
rise up from beneath the earth's surface was incredible. They
towered above their group like giant tombstones with jagged tops.
The moonlight filtered through the trees and backlit the stones, darkening the shadows in the clearing.

Alastair seemed to understand her wonder because he gave her a
warm smile from where he stood across the way. She smiled back,
reveling in the shared power of their group. The electrical current
caused her hair to billow in the wind and goosebumps to stand at
attention on her entire body. The brilliant white light filling the space
between outstretched palms was awe-inspiring, and Holly wondered
if Quentin had ever witnessed anything of this magnitude. They
would have a lot to talk about after all was said and done.

The stones were roughly fifteen feet high and easily five feet in
width. Moss grew on the southernmost part of the rocks themselves,
but if one strained, they could make out symbols etched into the hard
surfaces of each stone. There were fourteen formations in total, and

she had to assume the number was as significant as the need for seven witches to resurrect them.

The spell had been in Latin based on the few words Holly recognized when she repeated the chant. Once the ground trembling ceased, Preston stopped speaking, and they all fell silent. The light flowing from palm to palm abruptly died out, but the energized feeling Holly experienced during the ceremony remained. It was as if she were a human live wire and her nerve endings were going insane. Her vision was sharper, as was her sense of smell and hearing. Colors around her were more vibrant, and the sounds of the forest were like music to her ears.

As they each moved from their places to prepare for the second half of their "Revive Aurora" plan, Holly crossed to the standing stone closest to her and rested her palm on the warm surface. She wasn't sure what she had expected to feel, but the continuous low vibration wasn't it. Tracing the grooves of the symbols, it occurred to her they might represent the elemental magic of each of the witches. The one she outlined appeared to be the mark for water. It was in the shape of a teardrop with ripples flowing out from the bottom of the droplet. The whole thing was encased in a circle, and as she ran her fingertip around the drop, a glowing light backlit the symbol itself.

"Did you see that?" She whipped around to the group and pointed. "Watch!" Once again, she traced the element and laughed when it lit beneath her touch. "How freaking cool is *that?*"

Her father moved to stand next to her. "Do it again, child."

She complied, and watched as the light flared brighter.

Alastair grabbed her hand. "Again."

This time, the color of the light shifted from blue to a bright golden yellow and pulsed.

"Preston, GiGi! Have you ever seen anything like this?" he asked his siblings.

"It's miraculous," Preston breathed. "Obviously, I've touched the stones the first time I saw them, but I never thought to trace the elements."

Holly laughed and hugged her uncle. "I think it's a girl thing."

Preston stared down at her in wonder. "I believe that may be the first time you've ever hugged me."

"Now that's sad," she said and meant it. Wrapping her arms around his middle, she squeezed. "I'm sorry if I was ever standoffish to you, Uncle Preston. It was never intentional."

Quentin stood outside the circle, close to where they were. "She's a prickly pear, Mr. Thorne. It's her nature."

She giggled and blew her husband a kiss. "You wouldn't have me any other way."

Love burned brightly and lightened the irises of his dark, bedroom eyes. "I'd have you on any terms, Hol."

The smile started from the deepest part of her and spread out from there. "Quick, come see this."

Quentin looked to Alastair for permission to enter the circle. When her father nodded, her husband joined her and faced the stone. With her left hand, Holly reached for him and laced their fingers together. With her right, she traced the water element. To the surprise of everyone, all the symbols on the standing stone lit like a Christmas tree and remained glowing.

"Holy shit!" Quentin breathed. "That's badass."

Alastair sighed and slapped Quentin on the shoulder. "Son, you have a way with words."

Preston coughed into his hand to hide his chuckle.

Nash stood a short distance away, examining another stone. "The main element on this one appears to be wind. Winnie, will you and Zane repeat what Holly and Quentin did?"

Winnie waited for her fiancé to join her, then stepped up to the looming rock. Without hesitation, they joined hands, and Winnie traced the symbol. Once again, the entire stone flared bright and stayed lit.

"Quickly, find the fire and earth elements. Let's see what these will all do when awakened," Nash urged.

"Should we mess with things we know nothing about?" Summer asked. "Not to be a Debbie Downer or anything, but what happens if we light them all? Are we bringing down the wrath of the Gods?

Calling aliens from outer space?" The uneasy expression on her face made their sisters hesitate to take action.

As one, they all looked to Spring. She was the family encyclopedia and knew their spellbook from front to back. If anyone would have knowledge of these stones, it would be her.

Spring latched onto Knox's hand and pulled him to the stone that represented earth. "Only one way to find out." Like the other two, this formation lit up.

"I'm with you, sweetheart. I feel like this is a bad idea." Coop said as he joined Summer next to the standing stone directly across from Holly and Quentin. As sheriff of the small town of Leiper's Fork, Tennessee, Cooper Carlyle was programmed to believe anything that didn't follow official guidelines was bad. Holly understood his reticence, but her sister was a little more inclined to break the rules now and again. There were times she needed a bit of encouragement.

That encouragement came in the form of Autumn, who stepped up, forcefully joined Coop's and Summer's hands, then slapped Summer's other hand on the stone. "Don't be a chickenshit. If it wasn't meant to happen, we wouldn't have the power to make it so, now would we?" In a very Autumn move, she spun away, faced her open-mouthed family, and shrugged. "What? You were all thinking it."

Quentin snorted his mirth from beside her. "I adore your sister, love. She takes no prisoners."

"Yeah, she's a bit scary," Keaton muttered from behind them. "I'd better get my ass over there before she loses her shit. Those pregnancy hormones have made her unpredictable." He hurried to join his wife. With a wide smile—which Holly suspected was for show—Keaton lifted their joined hands and kissed Autumn's knuckles. "No lack of balls here, babe."

Autumn grinned and duckwalked to the rock with the fire element.

One by one, they each repeated the actions until all the stones were illuminated. A low hum started when the final one was brought to life.

"What did I tell you?" Summer ranted. "NASA is going to be all over our shit for this. Mark my words."

"She's going to love swearing without the resulting mice," Holly murmured to Quentin.

Nash stepped forward. "Okay, new plan. Our original idea was to have the sisters surrounding Aurora at the altar. Now, in addition to that, I'd like everyone else to position themselves in an outer ring. We'll create a circle within a circle within a circle."

Alastair frowned and moved to the nearest standing stone. He remained quiet as he studied the carvings. "Nash, do you remember anything from the *Book of Thoth* you traded to Isis?"

"Are you referring to the reference to the sacred etchings?"

"Yes."

"Of course!" Nash laughed and clapped his father on the back. "This is similar to the Egyptian's *Devine Ceremony* in the book."

"Exactly. I believe Isis wanted that book to thwart us from doing this very thing. But why?"

"That's not good," Holly muttered. She glanced up at Quentin and saw the unease on his face. Indeed, everyone suddenly appeared concerned. Or everyone but Spring, who sauntered to where Nash and Alastair conferred over the possible cataclysmic problems they could cause.

"The *Book of Thoth*? I know that book."

She held everyone's rapt attention as she slowly spun and studied the stones. The curious frown cleared from her brow as she smiled her triumph. "We won't cause the end of the world. But what it can do is open a portal to the Otherworld and the realms of the gods and goddesses. It had to be why Isis wanted the book—to prevent that from happening." She faced Alastair. "She wouldn't want any one mortal to have that power."

Knox ran a hand through his long, blond hair. "Why not remove the book at any time? She has the ability."

"I don't know. Maybe it had to be freely given? The answer lies with her. But what I do know is that we have the ability to bring Mother back with very little effort."

"You brilliant, brilliant child," Alastair breathed. "Tell us what to do."

"If I remember correctly, there is a particular spell from the book that must be used after the lighting of the stones. Nash, do you know the Archaic Egyptian language?"

"I do."

"Good. We'll need it to open the gate between worlds. Is this West?" she asked as she walked in the opposite direction. "We are looking for the stone that represents the 'False Door' or 'Gate of the Gods.' It was believed that false doors were built into pyramids and tombs to allow people to call their loved ones back from the other side to interact with them. Typically they were represented by a smaller door than what was standard at the time. There would be red and black markings on or around it."

"Here!" Autumn exclaimed. "There's a red mark on the edge of this stone."

Autumn, Keaton, and Spring searched for a black mark but found nothing.

"What if the opening isn't the stone itself, but between the stones?" Zane asked. "The black mark could be on the adjoining stone."

"That would make sense," Spring agreed. "Sometimes they weren't doors at all but a space between walls."

A thoughtful frown tugged at GiGi's brow as she joined her nieces by the westernmost standing stone. With a wave of her hand, the moss dissolved from the face of the rock, revealing the black slash they were looking for.

"Well done, sister," Preston applauded. "What's next, Spring?"

"Now we all line up on either side of the opening, creating a path directly to Mother."

"Like cheerleaders at a football game, welcoming players to the field," Ryker joked.

Spring laughed and nodded. "Exactly like that, Uncle."

Summer crossed her arms over her chest, and Holly recognized the stubborn pose. Spring's plan was about to be met with resistance.

"I don't like it," Summer told them all. "I'm not sure when *I* became the voice of reason, but who's to say what we might be letting through that opening? Isis took the book with the spell for a purpose."

Coop wrapped his arms around Summer from behind and pulled her to his chest. "Yeah, if I get a vote, I'm going with let's not do this."

"Anyone not on board may leave at any time," Alastair informed them all. His tone bordered on icy.

Yet Holly could see through the arrogance to the hurt beneath. Her father might never mention what he'd done for this family, but they all knew they owed him. She dropped Quentin's hand and moved forward. With a glare at Summer and Coop, she said, "We are *all* on board."

Although Summer's mouth tightened, she nodded her assent.

"Thank you, sister," Holly whispered as she hugged her.

"Yeah, well, if a fucking three-headed beast comes through that gate, it's on *your* head. And don't think I won't be pissed if it kills one of us."

Holly patted her twin's cheek because she knew it would annoy. "If a three-headed beast comes through that door, I have no doubt you could charm it into submission, Doctor Thorne, animal whisperer extraordinaire."

"Bite me."

"Enough clowning around. We are losing our window of opportunity here," Alastair said from Aurora's side. His focus was on her gray, still face. "We only have one chance at this, or she will be lost to us."

Preston joined him at the altar. "Then we'd better get started and bring Rorie home."

The brothers shared a look of understanding.

"We'll stand here on either side of Aurora," Preston said. "The rest of you, line up."

They each did as ordered and stood in a row—seven on one side and six on the other. Alastair and Preston positioned themselves in the rear next to Aurora's body. Nash took up a spot by the front in order to start the spell.

"Are we really doing this?" Winnie whispered to Holly. "Because to be honest, I'm a little nervous."

Holly clasped hands with her sister and squeezed. "Me too."

In reality, nervous didn't begin to describe the riot of emotions ricocheting around her insides. They could either be in deep shit with Isis and the rest of the Gods and Goddesses, or they might pull this off only to bring forth unsavory characters without reviving their mother at all. It was enough for a girl to develop an ulcer.

As Nash spoke the foreign words to open the gate to the Otherworld, an eerie silence fell over the group. Each person was secretly anticipating trouble and gearing up for what would happen next—or at least it seemed that way to Holly's active imagination. She was glad Knox and Quentin took the lead in their line. Both men had the favor of goddesses. It didn't hurt that they were the perfect eye candy. Who could be mad at a man who looked like either of them?

Nash abruptly stopped speaking, and a loud sizzling pop, like that from a fireworks display, echoed around the clearing. Holly's ears started to ring. The light from the standing stones blazed to blinding, and she was forced to close her eyes or risk burning her corneas. A high-pitched whining began, and the ground rumbled beneath their feet.

Quentin's grip tightened on hers.

"Whatever you do, don't break the chain!" Spring shouted over the noise. "Not until Mother is on this side and Nash closes the gate!"

Easier said than done when all Holly wanted to do was put her hands over her ears to drown out the deafening sound.

"Conjure earplugs if you need to," Quentin yelled to her, sensing her pain.

Right when she thought her eardrums would explode, all noise ceased, and the mystical light faded to a pulsing glow. Aurora Fennell-Thorne stood in the opening between the stones.

Holly gasped to see her mother looking so hale and hearty, but a part of her recognized this was only the spirit of her mother. Aurora's physical form lay on a stone slab fifteen feet away.

Aurora looked confused as she swayed in the gateway between worlds. It was as if she didn't recognize the faces around her. Alastair must have understood her dilemma because he called out to her.

The beatific smile on her mother's face when she saw him was breathtaking to behold. Reaching out, she opened her mouth to speak. Suddenly, she arched her back and her head fell back with her mouth open in a silent scream. Her lovely face contorted in pain as she dropped to her knees.

Holly tried to rush forward, but Quentin and Winnie held her tight.

"No!" Spring shouted. "Hold the line until Nash closes the gate." She nodded to Nash. "Now!"

Once more he spoke a foreign spell, and like a zipper, the opening sealed shut with the spirit of Aurora on the earthly plane.

"Circle behind her and guide her to her body," GiGi ordered.

They all closed ranks behind Aurora, mentally willing her to return to her body.

As Holly watched, Autumn took Keaton's hand and guided it to Summer's. "Hold tight, I have an idea." She ducked into the circle and knelt in front of their mother. "You know me, Mama. I know you do. We spoke in the Otherworld, remember?" Aurora held out a shaky hand as if to touch Autumn's face. "That's right, Mama. It's me. It's Autumn. Come home now."

Aurora looked to her body and back to Autumn.

Holly's heart sped up and her stomach flipped. Hope blossomed in her chest. Autumn was getting through.

"Rorie," Alastair rasped. "It's time to come home to me. To us."

CHAPTER 24

*A*s the dawn glimmered through the trees, Quentin cuddled Holly closer and drew the blanket more snugly around them. They could easily have used magic to warm themselves, but there were times it was nice to experience the early morning chill of fall.

"Can you believe we pulled that off?" she asked him.

There was a sleepy quality to her voice, and he felt misgivings at not insisting she get straight to bed. In her condition, she was pushing the limits of her health.

"I can feel your worry, Quentin. I'm fine. Witches are hardier than most."

"But not immortal."

"True, but I'm fine. Promise."

He kissed the cherry-red lips she turned up to him. "Okay. And to answer your question, no. That was insane."

"It's odd to sit here and see the clearing this still and calm as if nothing ever happened and giant standing stones weren't there only two hours ago."

"I know." He'd scarcely had a moment to process the events that went down in Athens before last night's chaos.

"You know what I want?"

"What?"

"Pie from that diner in town."

Quentin almost laughed. In the current timeline since the Beau and Michelle incident had never happened, Holly had never waitressed in that dump downtown. Although, he had to admit it was weird that the place was hopping this go around. Perhaps it was because Pete was never in charge of the kitchens and food was served in a timely manner.

"Pie, huh?"

"Mmm. Cherry with a ton of homemade whipped cream."

"I could conjure it for you."

"I could conjure it too, but where's the fun in that?" She lifted her head and grinned. "I thought we were being average mortals today. No magic, no drama."

"I need a little magic to boost my energy. I'm working on empty, love."

"We can go home if you'd like."

"No. If my prickly pear wants pie, she'll have pie." He shifted her to stand, then pulled her to her feet. "Come on. Let's head to town."

They were heading down the path toward Alastair's mansion when a shiver of unease danced across Quentin's mind. "Hol—"

"I feel it, too," she whispered and tightened her fingers over his. "Teleport us home."

As his cells warmed, he caught movement in the trees. "Stay here."

"No, Quentin. Don't go in there alone. It's not safe."

"I'll be fine, love. But stay here."

He jogged through the trees. A short distance away, he jerked to a halt when he saw who stood there.

Holly hollered his name from the path.

"I'm okay, Hol. I'm fine." The image of a woman and teenaged girl shimmered and disappeared, leaving him shaken. He was certain it had been Holly standing there in the woods. Did his gift as a Traveler allow him to see future timelines without trying? What did it all mean? Why had she looked thin and distraught?

Quentin only wished he'd had a chance to talk to her. To find out what was going on and help in some small way. He was slow to return to where he'd left a pregnant Holly, fuming on the path.

"That was reckless, Quentin. Please, take me home."

They were in their living room when Holly commented, "I think someone was in the woods. Someone saw us teleport."

"I saw them, too, love. I want to go back and check it out, but I need you to stay here."

She latched onto his arm. "No way! You aren't going back alone."

"Holly—"

"No! We'll call my father, and he can check the monitors of his security system."

Because her words were coated with an edge of hysteria, Quentin agreed. "Go lie down, and I'll ring your dad."

"Don't you dare go back, Quentin. I swear, if you do, I'm going to cut you."

He laughed and squeezed her tight. "I promise I won't go back. Now get in bed."

As she walked away, he rubbed the space over his heart. He loved her so much it hurt sometimes. Or maybe he was still itchy from all they'd been through that night.

In the doorway of their bedroom, she turned around and opened her mouth to speak. A sharp bowie knife came from behind her and sliced down through the top of her chest and into her stomach.

"No! *No!*" Quentin ate up the short distance between them and grabbed the arm of the man wielding the knife as he made a second downward slash.

Beau Hill!

But Alastair said he'd removed the problem. How was it that Beau was in their home? *Their warded home!* And as the thought occurred to him, Quentin realized from whence his unease bubbled.

The wards on the house were down. A powerful being had removed the protection they had in place.

In one smooth move, almost an exact repeat from seven years before in their alternate timeline, he used his strength and Beau's own body's momentum to fling him across the room. As Beau sailed into the wall, Quentin waved a hand and sent the wicked blade deep into Beau's heart.

He didn't spare the dead man another glance but dropped to his knees beside Holly. History repeated itself, and the words he spoke were identical to the time before. *"Don't leave me, love. You hang on! You understand? You'd better hang on, Holly!"*

He was reaching down to put pressure on the wound when the air around him rippled.

Athena's voice came to him. "Don't touch her, child. The blade was poisoned."

"I have to save her! I have to—"

"You have the power within you now. Remember the gift I gave you in the vault."

"The gift..." *The scroll she embedded under his skin!* "Thank you, Exalted One. I shall be forever in your debt."

"Hurry. You must reverse time before the last breath leaves her body." Her voice faded away.

Quentin ran for the grimoire she'd given him. He found the bookmarked page and started to recite the Traveler's spell. An excruciating burning started in his chest. With each word he uttered, the image of the owl branded into his skin became brighter, until it seared a hole in the fabric of his shirt.

Just when he thought he would pass out from such savage pain, the owl mark cooled, and he opened his eyes to find himself in the living room of their home. He heard a noise in the bedroom, but didn't have time to react as Past Quentin showed up with Holly.

"What the fuck?"

"Quentin? What?"

He held up a hand to urge caution to his shell-shocked twin self and his wife where they stood in the middle of the room. With a hand signal, he got the message across that there was an intruder in the bedroom. When he turned to take care of the problem, both timelines snapped together and he merged with his other self.

Holly's face registered her shock as she clung to him.

"Stay here," he whispered. "There's an intruder in the house."

"But the wards—"

"Are down," he told her in a hushed voice. "I mean it Hol, stay right here and don't move. Stay alert. Be ready to kill him if need be."

She remained behind as he kicked off his shoes and padded, silent as a ninja, toward the bedroom. Because he was prepared for the attack, he easily caught Beau's knife-wielding arm. Using Beau's momentum as he had the time before, he threw him across the room, denting the drywall.

Quentin charged. All the rage that had accumulated from the fear and pain of seeing Holly hurt were packed into his punches as he pummeled Beau's face.

"Quentin, you'll kill him!" Holly cried.

"Good!" He opened his mouth to say more, but dizziness assailed him. The room spun, the past and future became a kaleidoscope of images swirling about in his brain. Grabbing his head, he crashed to his knees. From the corner of his eye, he saw Beau reach for the blade.

"Holly, look out!"

But Beau didn't plunge the knife into Holly this time. No, the blade found a home in Quentin's chest, and the excruciating pain stole his breath.

"*No!* Quentin, no!"

Beau pulled the bowie knife free and turned his feral gaze on Holly.

"Teleport, Hol," Quentin croaked. "Get out now."

Her horrified gaze was locked on him, and she paid no heed to the psycho that was about to end both their lives.

"The baby," he gasped. "Save the baby."

Even as he held his hand to his chest in an attempt to stem the flow of blood, Quentin knew his time was up. He could feel the poison slithering through his bloodstream, destroying cells, killing him. A deep breath was impossible. He suspected a collapsed lung.

When Beau was almost within reach of Holly, she disappeared.

Like a rabid animal, Beau swung about and slashed wildly at thin air.

"You're f... fucked... buddy," Quentin panted with a half laugh. "S-so, fuck... ked." With zero energy and very little life force left, he rested his head against the wall where he knelt. "Al... Alastair is g... gonna tear you... you a new... ass."

He closed his eyes even as Beau stormed in his direction. A loud boom had his eyes snapping back open. Beau stood above him, blade poised to strike, but his attention was caught by the disturbance.

A simple twist of Quentin's wrist sent the knife plunging into Beau's throat. Seemed he did have the energy for one final bit of witchcraft.

Once again, Quentin shut his eyes. Holly would be okay. It was time for him to transition planes.

"Why did you do that, you foolish boy?" Alastair scolded as he squatted beside him. "I would have taken care of him."

He shot Alastair a mischievous grin. "I still... got it." His quip was ruined by his cry of pain. "Fuck me... this hurts. I can't... imagine how Holly... stood it."

"Holly?"

"Forgot... diff... different... time... line."

A flurry of activity around him kept him grounded for another moment or two more.

Holly's voice came from a long way away. *"Quentin, don't leave me, my love. You'd better hang on!"*

He would've snorted his amusement had he been able to drum up the energy or the oxygen. She'd used almost the same exact words he had when he tried to save her twice before.

"Don't... touch... me." He cracked his lids to meet her hurt gaze. "Poison... blade..."

Her hands flew to her mouth as if to hold back a scream, and she turned to her father in horror.

Alastair's grim expression didn't bode well for Quentin's long-term survival. He glanced at someone outside Quentin's peripheral. "Get your bag and ask Spring for a section of the plant." They all knew which plant he referred to. It was the only one capable of neutralizing the poison.

Father and daughter made eye contact before Alastair turned his gaze on Quentin again. "Son, I'm going to lift you and take you to the sofa. GiGi will be back shortly, and she's going to heal you. I want you to concentrate on breathing in and out on the count of three. Like this." He demonstrated slow, short inhales and exhales.

Quentin found the instruction helped, but only marginally. His chest hurt like a bitch. It was doubtful GiGi would be able to fix him up with a tin of Altoids this time.

"Tell me what happened, child," Alastair ordered Holly.

She gave him a rundown of the event.

Alastair gazed at Quentin thoughtfully. "You have the power to go through time at will?"

"Yeah... Athena... gifted it..."

"Are you the Quentin from the clearing that day? The one who gave me the note from myself?"

Quentin found his lips quirking. The pain was receding and in its place was a lightheadedness that felt like being in a drunken euphoria. "Yes... you should... have seen... your... face." He tried the trick of inhaling to the count of three but only managed two. "Keeping... that image."

"We have to do something." Holly was frantic from where she knelt at his side. "He's fading, Dad."

"Heart... of... Artemis..." Quentin panted. "Athena... says... will... help."

Alastair's brows shot halfway up his forehead. "You're in touch with Athena right now?"

"She's... here."

"He must be half in and out of each world to see her," Alastair murmured. "Holly, child, go to my estate and ask Alfred for the suit coat I was wearing in the clearing. I slipped the globe into my pocket before taking Rorie home."

In a blink, Holly was gone.

"Thank you for what you did tonight, son. You saved my little girl. I won't forget that."

"Love… her…" Quentin cracked his eyelids as wide as he could manage. "No… choice."

"Still, I am indebted. At anytime in the future, should you need me, I will be there."

He wanted to laugh at Alastair's earnestness and crazy belief that he might have a future, but it would cost him too much. Instead, he smiled and closed his eyes. It wouldn't hurt to sleep now. Holly was safe from Beau forever.

CHAPTER 25

*T*he day of Quentin's funeral, the sun dawned bright and beautiful in direct contrast to Holly's shriveled soul. Both Holly and GiGi had been too late with the tools to save him. She would never forget the peaceful smile on his still face. Never forget the devastation, or the desire to go with him.

Although Holly had summoned and begged her, Isis hadn't been inclined to grant any favors after their stunt in the clearing. When they used a spell from the *Book of Thoth* to bring Aurora back, they broke trust with Isis.

No, her beloved Quentin, with his mussy dark hair and milk-chocolate-colored eyes that promised sin, was gone. His body now encased by the black casket before her.

Dry-eyed, she stared as the coffin was lowered into the ground. She'd spent the last four days crying her heart out, but she had no more tears left. She was depleted. All emotion had exited her life, leaving only a deep, dark depression along with a burning anger that Quentin had left her alone. Goddess, how she hated to be alone.

Sharp pain announced the first contraction of her abdomen. Most of the night before, she'd felt restless; her nesting instinct had kicked in around midnight. Her baby would likely be born this evening.

Quentin would miss the birth of the child he'd longed to welcome to the world. With the third contraction, she sucked in her breath and swayed.

Her father's arm came around her shoulders, and she ducked out of his embrace. "Don't touch me," she snarled. "Don't you ever touch me."

"As you wish. Shall I conjure you a chair?"

"Cut the solicitous act. This is *your* fault. No amount of concern on your part can change the fact that my husband is lying..." Holly's voice broke in her fury. She took a deep, steadying breath. "...is lying there because of you and Victor Salinger. Because of a stupid-ass war you both engaged in years ago that is now carrying over to the next generation."

Her hand went to her baby bump. "And most likely to the next one after ours. You all disgust me."

"Be that as it may, Holly Anne, you've started your labor, and you need assistance."

"I'll go to a regular hospital like every other mortal."

"No, you won't," he countered. "It's too dangerous."

"You know what's dangerous, *Dad?* Being related to *you*. Being anywhere in your general vicinity. That's what's dangerous." She hissed at the pain of a stronger contraction.

A muscle ticked in his angular jaw. Her words had cut him to the quick, as she'd intended. Maybe if he could experience a fraction of the heartbreak and desolation she was feeling... but no, he'd have to care about anything and anyone other than her mother for that.

"Why are you here?" she asked tiredly.

"I cared about him, too, child. You may not believe it, but it's true." He raised his eyes skyward and took a long, deep breath. "I don't know anyone who didn't adore your young man. But mainly, I'm here for you."

"For me? That's a laugh. After this ceremony is over, I never want to see you again. I never want you to have a thing to do with my child's life. And if you defy me, Father, I'll rain hell down upon you the likes that make Zhu Lin and Victor Salinger look like your best friends."

Holly stumbled forward to where the coffin lay firmly seated in the ground. Because she was the size of a small barn, she couldn't bend. Instead, she called a clump of dirt to her. With cold deliberation, she dumped it in the eight-foot by three-foot hole.

"Goodbye, my love," she whispered.

Not bothering to spare any of her family a glance, she teleported to her home on Yellow Creek Mountain to collect the two suitcases containing clothes for her and the baby along with a small assortment of odds and ends.

Perhaps one day she'd return to the home she'd shared with Quentin, but right now she couldn't be here. Couldn't sleep in their bed, or see the couch they'd cuddled on at night. Couldn't bear to see the baby's room that he'd designed and created with such love in his heart.

She had laughed at him when he physically painted the room, telling him a simple snap of his fingers would have done the job. He had only shot her a panty-melting grin and said, "I want to have a hand in making the space perfect for our daughter."

"What happens if it's a boy?" Holly had teased.

"You're going to have to trust me on this one, love."

And she had.

She touched the wall of the nursery closest to her. He'd done an excellent job with the color. The pale pink called Summer Crush was the perfect color for a baby girl.

Holly experienced a moment of uncertainty over her decision to leave their home, but firmed her resolve. There was no way she could live in this place anymore. On the other side of town, Beau Hill was being laid to rest by his family and friends. If she stayed, she'd be subject to those same people's constant regard and judgment. More importantly, her child would, too. And other than to wish that black-hearted bastard to the darkest pits of hell, Holly didn't care to think about him another second longer.

She planned to stay with Spring and Knox until the baby was a few months old. Then, she would make her way in the world. It would be necessary to bind Francesca's powers so Holly could raise her daughter like a normal child, shunning all things Thorne. Without the influence of magic or the curse that followed their family, her daughter might have a chance at a happy life.

With her suitcases in hand, she closed her eyes and envisioned the front porch of her sister's house. Her cells warmed and triggered a wicked kick from her soon-to-be-born child.

"Enough, you little troublemaker. You'll have your way in a little while, but I need to get where I'm going first, okay?"

Before she could finish her scold, she'd landed on her knees on Spring's doorstep, heralded by a loud thunk and a whoosh that signaled the breaking of her water. Her time was at hand.

The door swung open, and Knox was there. Gently, he lifted and secured her to his chest as if she were the greatest treasure known to man.

"I have you, Holly. GiGi and Winnie are waiting in your room."

"How...?"

"As closely as everyone was watching you at the service, it was easy to guess when your pains started."

"No secrets in this family, huh?" she managed through her panting, ignoring the pang of grief at the word service. "Knox, before... before we go inside... promise me you won't... call Alastair to come... no matter what."

He stared down at her with somber, all-seeing eyes. "If that's your wish, Holly, I'll honor it." When he saw his wife approaching, he lowered his voice and quickly asked, "Should anything happen to you, who should raise your child?"

The thought of not being there for her daughter was terrifying, but she understood the importance of the question. Things could go wrong.

"Summer and Cooper... with the stipulation Alastair goes nowhere... near my child."

"Understood."

"Thank you," she rushed out as another contraction hit.

GIGI THORNE-GILLESPIE gently smoothed back Holly's dark hair as she gazed down at her sleeping niece.

"Is she going to be all right, Auntie G?" Summer whispered the question so as not to disturb her twin or the baby.

"Physically, she'll bounce back like any healthy woman who gave birth. Mentally and emotionally? Maybe with time."

"Quentin was the one constant in her life. I can't believe he's gone."

GiGi blinked back the moisture building behind her lids. She knew about loss, both in love and of a child. The grief her darling niece was experiencing wasn't going away overnight. The rage she was feeling was all part of the process. If the Goddess was kind, she'd find a way to ease Holly's suffering and allow her to transition to acceptance in a speedy manner.

"Do you know why they were targeted by Beau Hill?"

GiGi smoothed and tucked the comforter around the tragic figure on the bed, then rose and took the baby from Summer to place her in her mother's arms. A simple softly spoken phrase put a protection spell around the mother and child and allowed them their much-needed sleep.

With a nod, GiGi guided Summer from the bedroom into the main living area where the rest of the Thornes—with the exception of Alastair and Aurora—waited.

"I imagine you are all dying to learn what happened. Autumn, conjure tea and cookies, and I'll tell everyone what I know."

As they gathered around, GiGi relayed the why of it all.

After the stabbing, Alastair had explained to her how the night Quentin broke into the museum vault, he teleported into the past to warn of the future danger to Holly. His request to Alastair had been to make sure Beau wasn't a threat to anyone. In that, her brother had failed.

The measures Alastair had taken weren't enough. He had confessed to setting Beau up. The local authorities found enough marijuana plants in Beau's basement to put him away for a great many years. In addition to the pot, he was busted for counterfeiting. Sheriff Wyatt Thorne and his daughter, Evelyn Thorne, who happened to be a federal agent, saw to it that Beau's case was airtight. Beau had been convicted of cultivating and selling drugs, along with passing the counterfeit bills. The judge, Elijah Gillespie—Ryker's cousin—threw the book at Beau and gave him the strictest sentence. The poor sod was scheduled to spend a good portion of his life behind bars.

What no one had anticipated was the riot at the prison, or the escape of two convicts. One had been caught immediately, but the other—Beau—managed to evade capture. He came after Holly in a vicious act of revenge against the Thornes, knowing they were behind setting him up, even if he never completely understood why. His hatred had festered to the point where an old enemy of the Thornes was able to manipulate him into orchestrating the riot.

She finished with, "That enemy was Victor Salinger. Through his network of spies, he must have learned Alastair had targeted Beau." She shrugged because it was all still unclear as of yet. "Victor's name wasn't in the visitor logbook leading up to Beau's escape, but Nash discovered security footage of Victor speaking with Beau moments before the riot began. And now, because everyone around Holly foolishly tried to protect her, Quentin is dead."

"Jesus!" Knox shook his head in wonder and pulled Spring close. "No wonder she's upset with him."

"There was no way to anticipate that Beau would escape," Summer protested. "Would Holly rather Dad have murdered him from the beginning?"

Autumn poured everyone another cup of tea, but this time, she produced a bottle of brandy and splashed a dollop into each porcelain cup. "It would have been better." The gasped responses earned their group a careless shrug. "You're all thinking it. Regardless, what's the plan to bring Quentin back?"

"There is no plan, Tums," Spring inserted. "When one crosses to the Otherworld and their body has been in a death state as long as Quentin's, there is no return."

"Bullshit! No one is truly gone. I was on the other side. Souls are everywhere, mingling about and waiting for reincarnation or to be revived."

"No, niece, I fear Spring is correct."

"Are you telling me that my sister has to spend the rest of her life alone, trying to be a single parent to her child, while Quentin resides in the Otherworld?" She shook her dark, auburn head. "I won't accept that."

Autumn's stubborn insistence that she was right reminded GiGi of her own mother. While the two women looked very different, Ruby Smythe-Thorne and Autumn possessed the same exact temperament: react first and ask questions later. There wasn't a human on the planet who had ever gotten the better of GiGi's mother, and if the woman put her mind to it, there wasn't anything she couldn't accomplish.

Preston, who had remained silent most of the evening, finally spoke. "It's not a matter of accepting, child. It just is. There isn't a damned thing to be done about it."

"But Dad—"

He held up a hand. "Autumn, you'll give her false hope." He downed the contents of his cup and rose. "Losing loved ones is a fact of life. Don't you think we..." He gestured between himself and GiGi. "...would have brought back our loved ones if we could have? Sometimes, regardless of how much you want to, you have to let people go. Holly has to grieve and move on. She will. She needs time, patience, and our support."

In this, GiGi agreed with him whole-heartedly. It was a primary reason she had been against her oldest brother reviving Aurora. The dead should stay dead. "Even if you could resurrect Quentin, child, he might not be whole. He could very well come back evil. How much worse would that be?"

"I didn't!" Autumn cried.

"Maybe evil is the wrong word, but are you going to deny that a part of you is darker than before?" Autumn had no comeback, and GiGi hated that she was proved right. Hated that she needed to put her beloved niece on the spot like that in front of her spouse and siblings. "Let her recover in her way, darling."

"It's so damned tragic," Winnie murmured as she clasped Autumn's hand. "She didn't deserve this."

GiGi shifted her gaze to stare at the bedroom door. "No, she didn't."

CHAPTER 26

THIRTEEN YEARS LATER...

"*Mom*, there's a lady here to see you!" Francesca Buchanan sang out. "She'll be out in a sec," she told the red-headed woman standing on her doorstep. Because her mother had never received a visitor in all the years Frankie was alive, her curiosity got the better of her. "Are you a friend of my mom's?"

An amused light flashed in the amber eyes of the woman in front of her. "Something like that, kid. You gonna let me in, or are you going to make me stand on the porch all day?"

Embarrassment caused a swarm of heat to flood Frankie's cheeks. "Come on in."

"Thanks." The woman looked around the interior of their home and raised her brows as if she were impressed. "Nice place."

"My mom likes restoring old homes. This is the latest one." Personally, Frankie hated it. Once her mother was finished with a project, it went on the market and they were moving again. Her mother's hobby forced Frankie to be homeschooled when all she wanted was to be like normal kids and go to a public school. Heck, she'd even settle for a private school if it meant interacting with other kids her own age. "She intends to put it up for sale, and then we'll be hitting the road again."

She wasn't sure why she said what she did, but the warm understanding and sympathy in the woman's eyes made her stomach hurt. It was as if she saw through Frankie's I-don't-care attitude to the truth.

"What's keeping your mom, do you suppose?"

"Prob'ly didn't hear me with her earbuds in. I'll get her."

"Francesca, do you like moving as much as you do?"

"No." It occurred to her that the woman was fishing, but she saw no point in lying. "How do you know my name? Who are you?"

"That was rude of me, wasn't it? I'm Autumn Thorne-Carlyle. Otherwise known as your Aunt Autumn."

Frankie sat. When her butt hit the hard surface of a chair, she gasped and scrambled up. There hadn't been a chair behind her when her knees gave way. "What the fuck? *Achoo!*"

Autumn clapped her hands and laughed. "Delightful! It happens to you, too."

"What does?"

"You sneeze when you swear—just like your mom."

"Mom never swears."

"Pfft. That she allows *you* to hear," she muttered and waved a hand as if to brush aside that whole topic. "Which room is your mother in? I'll go find her myself."

Frankie pointed and watched the hurricane that was her Aunt Autumn blow through the house. Her long strides ate up the distance. Although Frankie was tall for her age, she had to run to catch up.

"Holly! Get your ass out here, sister! It's your moment of reckoning." Autumn shouted as she sailed through the kitchen toward the back of the house. "Hol! I swear to the Goddess I am going to kick your ass for making me chase you all over hell and back. Get out here, you tool."

Frankie couldn't prevent the grin spreading across her face. She liked the idea of this badass chick as her aunt. "To the right," she volunteered.

"Thanks, kid."

When they found the room her mother was painting, Frankie

paused in the doorway. Autumn, on the other hand, didn't stop until she stood within a foot of Holly. With one elegant arm, she reached out and smacked Holly on the shoulder.

Startled, Holly screamed and flung paint all down the front of Autumn's designer duds.

"For the love of...!" Autumn looked fit to be tied, while Frankie's mother looked like she'd seen a ghost. "Seriously, sister? Manual labor when you could have this done with a snap of your fingers?"

Holly shot a panicked glance in Frankie's direction. "Go to your room, Francesca."

"But Mom!"

"Go."

Frankie stared, pissed at the unfairness of it all. She was about to open her mouth to argue again when her aunt snapped her fingers. The outfit she was wearing was once more pristine, as if it had never been doused with paint.

"Oh, for fuck's sake! *Achoo!*"

From behind the two women, a pecking started. Fearful and unable to wrap her mind around what was happening, Frankie eased to her left to stare in open-mouthed wonder at the black bird pecking at the glass. Certain her eyes were bugging from her head, she purposely blinked.

"Am I dreaming?" she whispered.

Holly tossed the roller down and whirled to face her sister. "Now look what you've done! She didn't know what we are!"

Auburn brows raised in challenge, Autumn leaned forward to within inches of Frankie's mom. "What *I* did? I'm not the one who took off without a word to anyone, cloaked my activities, and pretended my family didn't exist for thirteen years. *Thirteen years, Holly!*" Autumn stabbed her in the shoulder with her index finger. "I'm not the one who ran away, denying my sisters and parents the right to know my kid." The volume of her voice rose with her anger. "I'm not—"

"I wanted to forget, all right?" Holly shouted. Tears brightened her dark, tortured eyes. "I wanted to forget, Tums," she cried raggedly. "Everywhere I looked, he was there. I couldn't stay."

Autumn wrapped Frankie's mom in a tight embrace. "I get it, Hol. I do. But I don't understand why you didn't keep in touch." The raw quality to Autumn's voice hurt to hear. These sisters had a shared pain that Frankie knew nothing about.

"Is it about Daddy?" Frankie asked tentatively. "About the way he died?"

Her mother never spoke of her father. Other than to say he had died before Frankie was born, she wouldn't talk about him at all. She did allow a single framed photo for Frankie's nightstand, but other than that, no pictures of him existed in their house. It was as if her mother had turned off that part of her life. A part Frankie desperately wanted to know about. She was certain her father had been a great man. In her mind, he'd have been fun and loving. He had to be to make up for her mother's lack of emotion, didn't he?

Maybe it was because her aunt was in the room, but Frankie hoped this might be the moment her mother opened up. Once again, Holly turned mute on the subject of Quentin Buchanan.

Years of pent up frustration bubbled up, fueling the anger that was never far from the surface anymore. Why did her mom have to be such a bitch all the time?

"I'm not a baby. I deserve to know what happened to my dad!" Frankie shouted. "Stop treating me like a child!"

"Stop acting like one," her mother snapped back.

It was their same fight, day in and day out. Her mother was always on a mission to fix up one house or another without caring if Frankie existed. Other than to make sure her daughter was fed, did her schoolwork, and washed behind her ears, Holly didn't give two shits if Frankie was alive.

"I wish you were the one who died!" Frankie cried, tears burning her eyes and nasal passages.

Holly and Autumn sucked in their breaths.

"I hate you!"

Frankie ran. She wasn't sure where she was headed, and she

didn't care. She needed space from her mother. In her flight, her hip caught on the small side table in the hall, knocking it into the wall and dislodging the small pink globe resting on its stand.

Instinct kicked in as the glass ball rolled toward the edge, and Frankie caught it before it hit the ground. She cradled the small sphere to her chest as her tears poured faster.

"Francesca—"

"I want my dad," she sobbed. "I want h-him to be alive. I w-want to talk to him and know that s-someone cares about m-me!"

"Oh, baby!"

As her mother reached for her, all Frankie could think was that if only she could talk to her dad one time, then maybe she'd understand why her mother refused to love her.

The globe in her hand began to warm, almost to the point of burning. The heat caught her attention. Why was it glowing? She glanced up to see terror replace the concern on her mother's face.

"Frankie, put the globe down," she said frantically as she inched closer. "Do it now, baby."

The world started to tilt. Frankie's head felt like it was spinning out of control. The room rocked back and forth, starting slowly and picking up speed at a nauseating pace. Her mom touched her arm as light exploded from the ball through the ceiling. The house fell away. The only sensation Frankie could feel was her mother's claw-like grasp of her wrist.

The light died out, and the two of them were alone in a wooded area.

"What just happened?" she whispered.

"I'm not sure, but I think we teleported," her mom answered in a hushed tone.

"Teleported?"

"Baby, I need you to listen to me like you've never listened to me before. This is going to sound crazy, but I need you to believe me."

Fear caused her stomach to flip-flop. "Okay."

"I come from a long line of—" Her words trailed off. Shock took the place of the intense expression she'd sported a second before. "Quentin?"

The conversation between a man and woman drifted to them, becoming louder with each passing second.

"Pie, huh?"

"Mmm. Cherry with a ton of homemade whipped cream."

"I could conjure it for you."

"I could conjure it, too, but where's the fun in that? I thought we were being average mortals today. No magic, no drama."

"I need a little magic to boost my energy. I'm working on empty, love."

"We can go home if you'd like."

"No. If my prickly pear wants pie, she'll have pie. Come on. Let's head to town."

Frankie spun around and saw a dark-haired man laugh as he hauled a heavily pregnant woman to her feet. He bundled her up in a black and gray checkered blanket.

As Frankie and Holly watched, he stopped walking and looked in their direction.

They heard him start to speak, but he was cut off by the woman.

"Stay here," the man said.

"No, Quentin. Don't go in there alone. It's not safe."

"I'll be fine, love. But stay here."

Frankie looked between her mother and the pregnant woman. "It's you, Mom. How is that possible? If that's you, that must be… is that my dad?"

Holly didn't answer her. Instead, she stepped forward with her hand raised as if to touch the couple. "How can this be?" Her scream of *"Quentin!"* caught Frankie off guard. Caught the couple off guard too if the way her father jerked to a stop was any indication.

Confusion lit his face as he ping-ponged his gaze between the woman behind him and her mother. "Holly?"

The pregnant woman hollered his name.

"I'm okay, Hol. I'm fine," he called back. When he was within a few feet of their location, he stopped. "Holly?"

"Quentin! Ohmygod, Quentin!"

He turned to glance behind him once, then swirled his hand over his head. *"Celo!"*

"What did you do?" Frankie asked, catching his attention.

He grinned, and the warmth of his smile healed the cracks in her heart. What did any of this mean? Was she dreaming? Was this all wishful thinking on her part? She feared she was going to wake up with an emotionally distant mother who said things like, "That's nice, Francesca. Be sure to put your clothes in the hamper."

"Magic." The overly dramatic way he said it was emphasized by the wiggle of his brows. Frankie bit her lip to stem a giggle.

"I halted time and concealed our little group." He studied her; a sweeping glance over her dark, wavy hair and down the length of her entire body. Once again, he looked deep into her eyes. Did he see his own brown eyes reflected back? "What's your name, sweetheart?"

"Francesca Buchanan. But I like Frankie."

"Francesca, huh?" His gaze sharpened on her face before he turned to her mom. He stroked a finger down the bridge of Holly's nose. "What's going on, love? I'm guessing it's a spell to bring you and our daughter from the future. Want to tell me about it?"

"Oh, Quentin," Holly whispered. "I…" She shook her head and flung herself into his open arms.

"It's all right, Hol. I promise, whatever it is, it's going to be all right."

"But it's not!" Frankie cried. She wanted to pour out everything, but she didn't even know how he had died. "You…" She looked to her mom for support.

"Beau Hill is going to break into our house, Quentin. It's the morning after we revive my mom."

Her father's face turned whiter than snow. "What are you saying?"

"He stabbed you. We were unable to save you." Choked sobs shook her mother's too-thin frame.

Why had she not realized her mom was that skinny? Frankie tried to remember the times her mother had eaten over the last two days, and all she could recall was a few bites of a sandwich before her mom tossed the remainder of her food in the trash. Embarrassed by her recent behavior, Frankie rubbed small circles on her mom's back, wincing when she felt the boney outline of her spine.

"Jesus!" He drew back slightly when the woman in the clearing called his name. "I have to get back or you're—uh, she—yeah, this is whack!"

Her mom clutched his forearms. "Quentin, wait! Before you take me home, ask Aunt GiGi to make the antidote to Lin's poison. Promise me you will get it and keep it on you. Promise!"

Frankie's father never winced as her mother's tone rose to deafening. He seemed to find nothing out of the ordinary with them showing up like this in the clearing, and Frankie had to believe he was serious when he said all this was magic. What other explanation could there be?

Quentin's concerned gaze darted between Frankie and Holly and back again. Suddenly, as if flipping a switch, he smiled and drew her mom back into his arms. With his left arm, he pulled Frankie into their circle. She thought she would suffocate at the tightness of the embrace, but she didn't care. To be held by her dad—the man she'd always fantasized would love her without question—made her world complete.

Tears filled her eyes and trailed down her cheeks. In a jerky gesture, she wiped her face with her sleeve.

"I'll do whatever it takes to be with you forever, my prickly pear," he whispered fiercely to Holly. "Whatever it takes to be with you both," he added as if he sensed Frankie's need to be included.

"I love you, Quentin. And I miss you."

"Thanks for coming back for me, love. I promise your efforts won't be wasted."

In a surprise move, Frankie's mother latched onto her and kissed her brow. "You can thank your headstrong daughter. She's the one who gave us another chance."

He laughed, deep and full of pure delight. "Headstrong? Dare I say a rebel? Yeah, I wonder who she takes after." His chuckle deepened as he swept her mom into a dancer's dip. "See ya on the flip side, love. Keep my side of the bed warm. Oh, and eat a cinnamon roll or two. You're going to need to keep your energy up for when I return." With a sweet kiss and wink for her mom, Quentin Buchanan, the guy who was better than any dad she could have dreamed up, strode away toward her pregnant mother, who waited impatiently on the dirt path.

When her mom turned to her and laughed, she realized it was the first time she'd ever seen her mother carefree.

Frankie's chest ached to watch her father walk away. She opened her mouth to call out to him and tell him she loved him, but the world tilted on its axis. "Uh, mom?" She lifted the glowing globe to show Holly. "I think it's happening again."

CHAPTER 27

*H*olly woke, heart pounding, and reached toward Quentin's side of the bed. The sheets were cool to the touch, and the space was empty. She jerked upright and called out, "Quentin?"

A simple snap of her fingers dressed her in clean jeans and a t-shirt. Anxiety bubbled inside, causing a small knot of emotion in the back of her throat. She had to find her daughter. She had to find Quentin. The dream last night had been heart-wrenching, and she needed to make sure they were both safe and alive.

The delectable scent of cinnamon rolls and cooked bacon hit her as she reached the hallway leading to the kitchen. She paused to inhale. Surely, the smell meant things were all right in her world?

She rounded the corner to find father and daughter laughing and running around the large center island.

"Not cool, Dad! And so not funny!" Frankie hollered as she chased him with a black silicone spatula.

In an abrupt move, he pivoted and grabbed their daughter in a bear hug, blowing a loud raspberry against her cheek. "Ah, my heart, you have to admit it was a little funny."

Frankie giggled. "Okay, maybe a little. But you're making the next batch."

"The next batch?" Holly asked as she stepped forward.

"Yeah, Dad—"

"Hold that thought, Frankie," Quentin clamped a hand over their daughter's mouth and whispered in her ear before depositing her onto the counter. "I have to kiss my beautiful wife good morning."

"Aw, Dad!"

The disgusted expression on Frankie's face set them both to laughing.

Quentin ignored her and gathered Holly close. "Good morning, my prickly pear."

"Good morning, my darling husband." Their kiss was long and lingering with enough spice to cause her breath to hitch. She bit back a smile at the naughty grin on his face. "Where's the rest of our troop?"

"Your dad came by to take the boys fishing."

"Fishing, or off to terrorize Nash's kids?"

"Probably off to terrorize Nash's kids," he agreed with a chuckle and another kiss. "Frankie decided to keep me company and help cook you breakfast in bed. You happened to wake before we were finished." A soft understanding lit his eyes. "You had the nightmare again?"

"Yeah. But I'm okay now." Holly exhaled her stress and eyed the mess they'd made. "You both know I appreciate the effort, but wouldn't it be easier to conjure everything?"

They'd had this same argument every Mother's Day for the last thirteen years. Quentin would insist they should cook the non-magical way to show it was important.

"Pfft, as if your husband does anything the normal way, sister," Autumn said from the doorway.

"Aunt Tums! Chloe!" Frankie jumped from the counter and ran to hug the newcomers.

Chloe broke free to hug Holly. "You ready for our spa day, Aunt?"

"I will be after I have a bite of the delicious breakfast my darling daughter and husband made for me."

"Quentin, how about the next time you see Keaton, you tell him how you are showing him up with little things like this? Let him know I threatened to run away with you."

He gave Autumn a one-armed hug and laughed when she fanned her face. "I can do that, but are you sure you don't want to quit threatening and run away with me already?"

"I'm standing right here, you player!" Holly scolded. In honesty, she didn't mind the lighthearted teasing. Quentin was hers, as she was his. "Where are the others?"

"Summer said she and the girls would meet us at Dixie's Salon. Winnie was helping Spring change the little ones and said they would pop over as soon as they were done feeding them." Autumn's wicked laugh rent the air. "Knox, Coop, and Keaton are on kid duty. Should we film it?"

"Three warlocks and a couple of magical two-year-olds? What could possibly go wrong?" Quentin laughed.

"You guys are mean. Those poor Carlyles don't stand a chance." Holly tried to hold back her laughter and failed.

Frankie plated up their breakfast. "Is Grandma joining us, too?"

"Yep. Our Witch Club President declared it law."

There was a wistful expression in Frankie's eyes, and Holly suspected she knew what the deep emotion was: the need to belong to the group as a whole. "When is the next election for Honorary President of the Witch Club?" she asked. "I'd like to nominate Frankie to take a turn."

Her daughter turned shining eyes to her. "Really, Mom?"

"If Chloe doesn't mind you taking a turn, I don't see why not. I think you're old enough to start organizing fun events for our family." With a side glance at Quentin, she added, "And maybe start school in the fall."

"School? Public school?" Her voice rose with her excitement. "Do you mean it? Ohmygod, thank you! Thank you!"

"Thank your father. It was his idea."

Frankie flung herself into her father's outstretched arms. "Thank you, Daddy. Thank you so much! I promise not to use magic in public."

"I know you won't, my heart. I have the utmost faith in you. You remember why we keep what we are a secret, right?"

Holly knew he was referring to the time when their daughter triggered her gift, catapulting them back in time to warn him of impending danger. Although Holly had no recollection of the event herself, she still woke on occasion in a full-blown panic, having dreamed Quentin was lost to her forever. Quentin was always there with loving arms ready to chase her demons away. He had explained it was an echo from another timeline. A type of déjà vu.

Frankie had once said it was as if two sets of memories existed for her. The ones with her father, and the ones without. The haunted look that darkened her daughter's milk-chocolate eyes to black had convinced Holly, as nothing else had, that Frankie spoke the truth.

For Quentin, the understanding came easier. He seemed to comprehend what this meant and had earned his daughter's undying love when he thanked her time and again for saving his life.

Holly shoved away her train of thought and reached for another set of plates. "I'm assuming you and Chloe want a cinnamon roll since you showed up for breakfast the fifth Mother's Day in a row."

"Is the sky blue, sister? Besides, I like looking at your eye candy."

Quentin laughed and offered to remove his shirt while he cleaned the kitchen, earning himself a swat with the back of Holly's hand.

"Don't even think about it, you tool. That's for when Frankie and the boys are hanging with my dad and no one else is around."

Strong arms came around her waist from behind. "That's my beloved wife." He lowered his voice so only she could hear. "Why don't you send everyone ahead, and you and I can have alone time?"

Her breasts tightened, and her lady parts added their vote for alone time.

The mischievous expression in her sister's eyes said she knew exactly the effect Quentin's murmured words had on her.

Holly gave her the do-me-a-solid-and-take-the-kids-and-go look.

Autumn shrugged and grinned around a bite of cinnamon roll.

It was time to get aggressive with the eye gestures and facial twitches to indicate she meant business.

"You look like you're having a seizure, love. Play it cool and follow my lead."

The heat of embarrassment tinged her cheeks. Okay, maybe she had gone over the top.

"Frankie, my heart, your mother and I have something important that just came up—" Autumn's snigger earned her a quelling look from Holly, but the laughter in Quentin's tone was obvious when he continued. "—and we need you to head over to the salon with your aunt and cousin."

"But it's Mother's Day!" she objected.

"Right! Make sure you clean the kitchen before you go. I'm approving magic for clean-up duty. Have fun."

He didn't allow time for anyone to object; he simply teleported Holly and himself to their bedroom.

"Lie down on the bed and let me wake you properly, love."

Doing as he requested, she leaned back on her elbow and lifted a brow in challenge. "If you intend to do this properly, the sound will carry."

"Oh, I intend to do it as improperly as possible, my prickly pear." Quentin crawled over top of her, careful to brush and caress every inch of exposed skin he could. "But if you don't wish your cries of ecstasy to be heard by everyone, I suggest you utilize Granny Thorne's cloaking spell."

"Cries of ecstasy? That's a tall order for you to deliver on."

Drawing back, he met her gaze with a bold stare and a knowing smile on those lips made for sin.

Her breath caught in her chest. Yeah, he totally could deliver. "Fine, I'll say the—"

His kiss consumed her and scrambled her brain waves. When they came up for air, she'd forgotten the original topic of conversation. "What was I saying?"

His rich laughter was sunshine to her soul. "Never change, Hol. Never change." Absently, he waved a hand toward the door. *"Celo!"*

———

FRANKIE SMILED as her parents teleported to their bedroom. *As if she didn't know what they were doing in there!* Pfft! It didn't gross her out as it might other kids. Well, maybe if she thought about the actual *act*, it might. But when she witnessed them sneak away, she only saw their happiness.

Since they altered the timeline, her mother had been different. The only way to describe it? Her mother was now present. Instead of walking around with a sad, haunted look on her face, Holly Thorne-Buchanan now faced each day with a sparkle in her eye and a happy smile on her lips.

All because of Quentin.

He was everything Frankie had hoped he would be and more. The fun-loving side of his personality never allowed her to dwell on the alternate timeline when he wasn't around. His constant love and teasing attention made life picture perfect.

"We should go before those two start rocking the house," her aunt said. She popped the last piece of the ginormous cinnamon roll into her mouth and grinned. "Visualize a clean kitchen and let's go, kid."

"Think I can do it myself? Mom or Dad always helped me in the past."

"Girl, you are a Thorne Witch. Added to that, you're the great, great... well, you descend from Zeus. You have power beyond your imagination."

Frankie bit back a smile. Yeah, her lineage *was* pretty badass. Closing her eyes, she envisioned a platter for the leftover food. In her mind's eye, she warmed the food to steaming and placed a domed lid over the top—like a swanky hotel room service. Next, she mentally put the remaining dishes in the dishwasher and reset the table how her mother liked it.

Opening her eyes, she saw the results of her magic. "I did it!"

"Yeah, kid, you did. But you might want to get rid of the flour on your shirt."

"I used to send Mom and Dad mimosas when they would hide out in their bedroom. Just sayin'." Chloe laughed and kissed Frankie's cheek.

Autumn smiled and hugged her daughter tight. "You always were a wonderful child. Now you've grown into a beautiful woman. Twenty-two next Tuesday. I can't believe it."

"Yep, back to Harvard in the fall. I'm going to miss everyone."

"Will you still have Derek to keep you company?" Frankie added.

"No. He graduated this year. Besides, he still refuses to see me as anything other than his best friend."

"We'll have to rectify that," Autumn assured her. "But only *after* you've graduated."

Chloe's face fell. "No rectifying that, Mom. He's dating someone else."

"Boys are dumb," Frankie said, parroting her Aunt Tums's favorite saying.

"Exactly! Nothing a good firebombing of his truck won't cure." Autumn gave Frankie a quick tap on her butt. "Now, set that tray outside your parent's bedroom door and let's get going."

LOVE WHAT YOU'VE READ? Turn the page for an excerpt of LONG LOST MAGIC.

LONG LOST MAGIC EXCERPT

$\mathcal{T}$oday, like every day for the last month, Aurora Fennell-Thorne stared out over the thick cluster of trees surrounding her prison. She probably shouldn't consider the place her prison. Her jailor had offered her freedom since the day she woke from her coma six weeks ago. But where could she go?

The door opened behind her, and the air contracted.

It was always such when Alastair Thorne entered the room—blond and bold, ready to take on any challenge.

"I've brought you breakfast."

His voice was rich and deep with a heavy dose of arrogance. It curled around her and tickled something in the farthest reaches of her memory. Some long-lost glimmer of... what? Love? Already it was gone. She was no more than an empty shell with fragmented images dancing about her broken mind.

"Aurora, you must eat." The tone brooked no argument, and yet, she refused to give in to his demands. With a flick of her bony wrist, she used the small bit of magic at her disposal to knock the tray from his hands.

A ripple of anger tore at the fabric of the space around her. Hers? His?

"I'm quickly becoming tired of your tantrums, my love. Don't make me..." He trailed off.

She studied his reflection in the mirror over the dresser. His tortured, longing gaze struck another chord. His eyes connected with hers in the glass, and his already sapphire gaze darkened to midnight blue.

"Your daughters want to visit today. Would you care to see them? Holly would like to show you your new granddaughter."

She broke the hold by tearing her gaze away and resuming her study of the endless forest beyond the windowpane.

"Aurora, I asked you a question."

She gave a negative shake of her head and went back to ignoring him.

"If you don't allow them to visit, they'll believe I'm keeping you against your will."

"You are," she rasped, her voice hoarse from disuse. Close to twenty years in stasis did that to a voice box.

"Do you not remember what we shared? Why you're here?"

"Go away," she croaked harshly.

She heard the heaviness of his sigh and the soft tread of his soles on the wood floor as he moved toward the exit.

His fingers snapped, and she jumped at the thundering sound it made in the silent room. From the corner of her eye, she spied the destroyed breakfast tray disappear along with the mess of food. Alastair used magic for most things, and cleaning the spills she created in her rage had no drain on his power. She wished it did so he could feel what it was like to be helpless.

Before he left, he cleared his throat. "I only want to help you, my love."

She whirled the wheelchair around and sneered in his direction. "Help me?" Anger gave her the energy and ability to spin the wheels in short bursts. It was enough to propel her to where he stood. She waved at her thin frame. "You did this to me, Alastair."

"*No!*" The very walls shook with the fury of his denial. With concerted effort, he calmed. "No, Aurora. I'm done taking the blame. If anything, I—"

"I hate you," she spat.

He reeled back at her vehement response. The expression on his face shifted from shock to bleak to resigned then to blank. "Very well. I'll hire a nurse for your care. You need not see me again."

With great dignity, he closed the door behind him. For several heartbeats, she stared, waiting for him to return and plead his case as he had nearly every day since she first rejected him. Her pulse hammered in her ears and made her deaf to any other sound.

Only this time, he didn't return.

She frowned and spun back around. Pausing, she took in the space as a whole. Goddess, she hated this damned room. Light and airy in direct contrast with her dark, heavy thoughts. Her eyes fell to the empty nightstand. Alastair had stopped refreshing the flowers and removed the vase on the day she could finally voice her complaint about the cloying smell of the roses.

He'd brought her calla lilies that same afternoon. She'd insisted he remove those as well. Insisted he remove the book of poems and anything else of a romantic nature from her presence.

She didn't want to be surrounded by lively, loving things when she was dead inside.

ALASTAIR SANK into the plush leather upholstered chair before the fire, Cognac in hand. He took a long sip of the liquid without removing his gaze from the dancing flames.

Christ, what had his life become? Nursemaid to a woman who hated him. Before that, a pathetic excuse for a man. One who had believed, in the end, love would conquer all. One who'd moved heaven and earth to bring his mate back from the brink of death. One who did things any other human being with a conscience would cringe at doing. One who hated himself most days.

With another heavy sigh, he rested his head back against the chair.

Now, he had the Witches' Council on his ass, ready to strip his powers. Or at least attempt to. He snorted. He'd like to see them try. No one was as powerful as a Thorne warlock.

Except Knox Carlyle and Quentin Buchanan, a little voice whispered.

Yes, but he doubted either would take up arms against him. They were mild-mannered men who only lived to love their women. Thorne women. They wouldn't rock the boat.

A flicker of light appeared in the center of the room—an indication of an incoming witch. Only two knew what the interior of his study looked like and, as a result, could teleport in without harm.

A blonde woman appeared, beautiful and slightly rumpled, with color high on her cheeks. Her eyes, bright blue and questioning, sought him out.

Summer.

"Father."

"Daughter," he said with a slight twist of his lips at her formal tone. She'd grown up believing Alastair's brother, Preston, was her real father. Since learning the truth, the poor dear was still trying to figure him out.

Her gaze fell to the tumbler in his hand, and a pained look crossed her features. "She still being difficult?"

"How ever did you guess?" he mocked as he lifted the glass.

"What can I do to help?"

"I don't know if there is anything you can do. She's bitter because her powers didn't fully return when she woke." His mouth curled in a self-disgusted grimace. "I'm sure she only wants them in order to be away from me."

"I'm sorry."

Because she actually sounded as if she meant it, he said, "Thank you, child."

"I'm assuming she doesn't want to meet any of us? See the women we've grown into?"

He started to shake his head and paused. An idea formed and brought with it a smile. Summer might be able to spend time with her mother after all.

FROM THE AUTHOR...

Thank you for taking the time to read *REKINDLED MAGIC*. If you love what you've read, please leave a brief review. To find out about what's happening next in the world of The Thorne Witches, be sure to subscribe my newsletter.

Subscribe: www.tmcromer.com/newsletter

Books in The Thorne Witches Series:

SUMMER MAGIC
AUTUMN MAGIC
WINTER MAGIC
SPRING MAGIC
REKINDLED MAGIC
LONG LOST MAGIC
FOREVER MAGIC
ESSENTIAL MAGIC

You can find my online media sites here:

Website: www.tmcromer.com

Facebook: www.facebook.com/tmcromer

TM Cromer's Reader Group: www.facebook.com/groups/tmcromer-fanpage

Twitter: www.twitter.com/tmcromer

Instagram: www.instagram.com/tmcromer

How to stay up-to-date on releases, news and other events...

✓ *Join my mailing list. My newsletter is filled with news on current releases, potential sales, new-to-you author introductions, and contests each month. But if it gets to be too much, you can unsubscribe at any time. Your information will always be kept private. No spam here!*
www. tmcromer.com/newsletter

✓ *Sign up for text alerts. This is a great way to get a quick, no-nonsense message for when my books are released or go on sale. These texts are no more frequently than every few months. Text TMCBOOKS to 24587.*

✓ *Follow me on BookBub. If you are into the quick notification method, this one is perfect. They notify you when a new book is released. No long email to read, just a simple "Hey, T.M.'s book is out today!" www.bookbub.com/authors/t-m-cromer*

✓ *Follow me on retailer sites. If you buy most of your books in digital format, this is a perfect way to stay current on my new releases. Again, like BookBub, it is a simple release-day notification.*

✓ *Join my Facebook Reader Group. While the standard pages and profiles on Facebook are not always the most reliable, I have created a group for fans who like to interact. This group entitles readers to*

"reader group only" contests, as well as an exclusive first look at covers, excerpts and more. The Reader Group is the most fun way to follow yet! I hope to see you there!
www.facebook.com/groups/tmcromerfanpage

CPSIA information can be obtained
at www.ICGtesting.com
Printed in the USA
LVHW021059090520
654944LV00004B/343